I0628592

THE ASTEROID
MURDER CASE

The murder of UN observer Carl Neal on a lonely outpost of the Asteroid Belt would seem to be only a small human tragedy, and yet it opens up vistas both of millennia of time and of unimaginable distances.

Inspector Tom Dooley, Chief of Security of the American Sector of the Belt, together with his faithful "Watson," Ralph Phelps, must sift through the many clues to unravel the mystery of Neal's death. Here is a first-rate science fiction adventure, combined with a classic murder mystery!

Borgo Press Books by ARTHUR JEAN COX

The Asteroid Murder Case: A Science Fiction Mystery
A Collector of Ambroses and Other Rare Items

THE ASTEROID MURDER CASE

A SCIENCE FICTION MYSTERY

ARTHUR JEAN COX

Based on a Story by Ross Rocklynne

THE BORGO PRESS
MMXI

THE ASTEROID MURDER CASE

Copyright © 2011 by Arthur Jean Cox

FIRST EDITION

Published by Wildside Press LLC

www.wildsidebooks.com

DEDICATION

Dedicated to Ross Rocklynne's most cherished
friend, **Minnie Enos**—

Where she is, there is a
gentle breeze from Golgonooza.

CONTENTS

INTRODUCTION
HOW THIS BOOK CAME TO BE

Ross Rocklynne was a frequent contributor to the pulp science fiction magazines that flourished during the long middle stretch of the twentieth century (from the 1930s into, say, the 1960s), and he remains today one of the most fondly remembered names of that period. He published more than 100 stories, the two most famous being "The Men in the Mirror" (1938) and "Time Wants a Skeleton" (1941), both of which appeared in the premier magazine of the field, *Astounding Science Fiction*— and both of which, it should be noted, take place in the Asteroid Belt.

The story here has grown out of a much shorter one Ross wrote towards the end of his career. He had meant it to be published in *Analog* (as *Astounding* had now become), but its editor, the titanic John W. Campbell, returned it, saying that "science fiction and mystery fiction are incompatible." Ross's disappointment was compounded by its also being returned by the less venerable but much respected *Galaxy*; but he held fast to his belief that "The Asteroid Murder Case" was worthy of publication.

He asked me to read it and comment on it. My advice was that he should expand it into a novel, for it seemed to me that the science-fictional setting could not be satisfactorily explored, nor justice done to the murder mystery story-line, in a mere 13,000 words. We were discussing all this, with an eye to collaborating on the larger version, when, a few days later, near the end of

October of 1988, Ross very unexpectedly died. He had been my closest friend for more than twenty years.

Those familiar with what is now called the Golden Age of Science Fiction may have noticed that Ross was very much at home in the Asteroid Belt. He wrote at least eight stories set against that shifting, fragmented landscape, surely more than any other writer of that time or since. It had occurred to me more than once over the years that the posthumous publication of "The Asteroid Murder Case" would be, should be and perhaps, if revised and enlarged, could be a fitting capstone to such a career. Reflecting further, I found that what I would most like to do would be to take Ross's spurned and forgotten tale and transform it into The Quintessential Ross Rocklynne Asteroid Story. That may seem a challenging, even a vaunting, ambition—and it is; but how, after recognizing the desirability of doing such a thing, could I not make the attempt? Any question as to whether I have succeeded in that attempt must be left to the reader to decide.

I should add, after the above, that I have of course retained Ross's characters, settings, and main story-line; but I have embroidered freely and without hesitation, incorporating into the story several new elements, of which I think that he—who had less of the writer's usual vanity than any other writer I've met—would have approved. These include a new character who looms rather large in the last few chapters and who of course cannot be named at this point.

And, finally, a confession: as I worked on the script, I had in mind a secret purpose, and that was to produce a story that could be enjoyed by readers today, but which the readers of *Startling Stories* in 1945—that is to say, in Ross's heyday—would not have considered out of place in the pages of that magazine. I hope that those imagined readers would have found the story as much fun to read as I have found it to write.

I extend that hope to any and all actual readers.

I would like to thank Keith Rocklin for his generous permission to publish his father's old story in its present form.

—Arthur Jean Cox
Los Angeles, California
June 2011

CHAPTER ONE

The two men entered the igloo. Seen from a distance they might have been taken, with their parka-like headgear, for Eskimos; or, perhaps, with their white suits and backpacks, for arctic explorers. But they were neither, and the environment they braved was even less hospitable than that of Earth's polar regions.

Five other men, dressed like the first two, dispersed around the exterior of the igloo, which was a white, reticulated, semi-flexible structure twenty feet long and a dozen feet wide. They moved with an oddly awkward grace: with a stately ponderousness, like elephants, although they seemed as light as feathers. The ground on which they so carefully placed their feet was hard, angular and choppy; and overhead, or, more accurately, all around, the stars were brilliant points of light, fixed and unwavering. One star in particular was distinctly larger than the rest and so very bright that one might almost have read a newspaper by it,

The two men who had pushed their way into the igloo through a series of airtight seals were Chief Inspector Thomas Dooley of the American Security forces stationed on Vesta and Ralph Phelps of the Asteroid Regulatory Commission. They found themselves in the dark, except for a dim glow like a nightlight to their left: probably meant to mark the location of the dwelling's commode.

A voice spoke beside Dooley's right ear. "We found it, Chief. It's at this end of the igloo, about five feet up. And it's large, almost half an inch across."

Dooley said, "Shine your light through it will you, Oreste?" He and Phelps looked to their right and saw a flash of light like a beacon. "Who's at the other end?"

"Me, Chief. Ito."

"Shine your light over that end, Ito—yes, there it is; also about five feet up. It must have just skimmed over the surface of the asteroid, probably at seven or eight miles a second. Can you find the light-switch, Phelps?"

Phelps could. It took their eyes some twenty seconds or more to adjust to the sudden glare; but before they had quite done so, both had seen the body on the bed.

Phelps said, "He's here all right."

"Well, where else would he be?" said Dooley, with a touch of asperity that was habitual with him. "His clodhopper is anchored not ten yards from the door. He couldn't have gotten far without it. Ito, Oreste, plug those holes. The rest of you see about getting some air back into this thing. Use the emergency tanks and equipment aboard the deceased's vehicle."

The body lying on the air-inflated mattress was that of a man of about forty: dark-haired but light-skinned...very light-skinned. His eyes were closed, but blood had oozed out from under the lids. Blood also had trickled from his nostrils and ears; his mouth, slightly open, was filled with a dark substance, probably congealed blood and stomach juices.

Phelps shuddered inside his suit. "Carl Neal. I knew him, you know. What an end to his life!"

Dooley said, "His conditioner couldn't cope with two holes that size at opposite ends of the tent. Too bad, but meteorites are one of the facts of life out here in the Belt. Fortunately, most of them are the size of pinheads or smaller."

"The drop in air-pressure didn't awaken him."

"No," said Dooley, "nor the decreasing oxygen supply. He adjusted to it at first as he slept and then was without sufficient iron in his blood to trigger him awake."

"Good thing his wife called the station. She knew something

was wrong, even though she was on Mars. Woman's intuition, I guess."

Dooley grunted. He looked around. The igloo was the standard one-roomer of the kind commonly used on asteroids. It had a kitchen-area, latrine, shower, a table, mattress, a video-console and, somewhat to his surprise, two blow-up easy chairs.

He said, "Not one, but two," indicating the chairs, which were almost visibly bulging at the seams because of the lack of external air pressure. "Now, *that's* luxury!"

The chairs in question faced each other across a flimsy table bolted to the floor. Playing cards were scattered on its surface, mostly in front of each chair. The cards were made of metal but, nevertheless, because of the negligible gravity, were being stirred by the air—a mixture of oxygen, carbon dioxide and water vapor—already flowing into the room through a hose inserted into the vent from outside.

"He had a visitor," said Phelps.

"It is permitted," said Dooley. He examined the cards. "The fellow on this side had the winning hand. But what's this?" He pointed to something scribbled on the white surface of the table. "Words? Gibberish? A code?"

Phelps studied the markings. "Looks like you could read it if you held it up to a mirror. My God!"—and he jumped six feet away from the table, despite his shoes, which would have weighed thirty pounds each on Earth.

For the inflated chair on which he had casually rested his right hand had moved. It was crumpling, shrinking, drawing down and back into itself. Both men stared, as if fascinated by its fatalistic shruggings and clumsy foldings.

Phelps said, "It's sprung a leak."

"No," said Dooley after a moment or two. "I don't think so." For the chair had reached a point of rest: it had stopped shrinking. And at the same moment Oreste's voice spoke again by Dooley's ear.

"Okay, Chief. The air pressure in there is a standard 14.7, at 54°. You can remove your helmets, if you like."

Dooley did so, with some feeling of relief. Actually, he was perfectly comfortable inside the NASA suit and helmet, but he much preferred talking to others face to face. The face and head he himself now exposed to view was craggy and rough-hewn—Oreste had once compared it to an asteroid, though not in his Chief's hearing—and it had a sizeable wedge of chin that suggested skepticism and, perhaps, stubbornness. He was almost a young man by modern standards, barely fifty as yet, and had achieved his present position as Chief of Security of the American Occupied Section of the Belt by virtue of intelligence and hard work. His friend Phelps followed his example: running his finger under the front of his helmet, as if he were pantomiming someone slitting his own throat, while pressing a safety release at his belt. Unlike Dooley, whose helmet was still attached at the back, he removed his entirely and deposited it on the table, revealing himself as a man a shade younger than Dooley and quite a few shades softer: his round face with its mop of sand-colored hair suggesting tolerance, good-humor, and complacency.

With their helmets detached, the two were out of automatic communication with the men outside the igloo and could have spoken to each other privately, if there had been any point in doing so. The air was sharp and chill, through not unpleasantly so, and as yet untainted by the body on the bed.

Both men, sharing the same thought, looked in that direction.

Phelps said, "I'm glad I'm not the one who has to tell her"— meaning the dead man's wife.

Dooley grunted again. A voice, tiny and sepulchral, like a cricket speaking from a bucket, sounded at his back. "Shall we come in now, Chief?"

He touched a button at his neckline. "No, I'm going to look around first." Releasing the button, he added for Phelp's benefit, "I'd better keep the three non-professionals out for a while. Not that they could trample on much evidence in this case."

He examined the kitchenette, the latrine, the shower. He pulled aside a curtain opposite the shower and discovered a spacesuit, a Westinghouse 1000 model, mounted on a rack, as well as some lesser articles of apparel. He stood there a moment; bent, pushed aside the suit, looked behind it, rummaged among the leotards.

When Dooley looked around again, Phelps saw that his friend's face was puzzled, suspicious, even scared. He asked, "What's wrong?"

Dooley didn't answer. He stood looking around the entire interior of the igloo for two or three minutes; then, retracing his previous steps, he poked again through the kitchenette, the latrine, the shower. As Phelps watched in growing puzzlement, Dooley's movements became faster, more violent. He opened a cabinet and tossed weighted pots and pans onto the seamless floor, pawed through a chest of linen and underwear, strewing them through the air, where they drifted and settled slowly as if under water. He was like a drunk searching desperately for a misplaced bottle of booze.

He gave up. He came slowly back towards Phelps. He sank down onto the half-inflated easy chair and seemed partly deflated himself. He squatted there, with his knees raised and his hands dangling between them.

He said, "I was supposed to leave for Earth in five days, to spend Christmas with my family in Indiana."

"What happened?" asked Phelps.

"An old-fashioned Christmas," said Dooley, speaking to the floor. "I'm not a sentimental man, but I've been looking forward to that for some time."

"What happened?"

"I was going to trim a tree with my father and mother. I was going to hang red and blue ornaments and striped candy canes on the branches and make chains of candied popcorn. And maybe, just maybe, I'd go out Christmas morning and throw snowballs at my sisters—did you know I have three sisters? Of course you did. And I have umpteen nieces and nephews, and they were all going to be there, every single one of them. And in the afternoon we'd all sit around in the living-room and eat turkey and sweet potatoes and pumpkin pie and digest them through under normal Earth gravity...."

"What the hell's wrong?" demanded Phelps, with unaccustomed force.

"No helmet," said Dooley, with profound weariness. "There's a spacesuit hanging on the wall back there, but there's no helmet with it. There's no helmet anywhere in the whole damned place. It's not here. And he couldn't have walked in from outside without a helmet. He must have been carried in." He raised his eyes, disgusted and angry, to those of Phelps. "He was dead before that hole was punched through the igloo. It wasn't an accident. It was murder."

CHAPTER TWO

When Dooley admitted his two subordinates and the three volunteers into the igloo, they saw nothing of what Phelps had just seen. He was not in the least despondent, but very energetically in command.

"You're to videograph every inch of this place, right down to the scratches on the pots and pans. Cyril, I particularly want a good shot of those markings on the table there. And I want you to photograph this half-collapsed chair from half a dozen contrasting angles. Ito, I want the fingerprints from the cards and table there and from those glasses in the washer. Oreste, when you removed the tanks from Neal's clodhopper, you didn't notice the helmet to a spacesuit inside the flyer, did you?"

"No, Chief, I didn't." Lieutenant Oreste was Dooley's second-in-command. He was a blond young man, who had been in the Asteroids such a short time that the sun-caused freckles across the bridge of his nose hadn't faded yet. He considered carefully. "The helmet to a spacesuit? Does that mean...?"

"Never mind what it means," said Dooley. He liked Oreste but had never seen any reason to specifically mention that to the younger man.

"Here's what I want you to do: I want you to measure the exact size—in millionths of an inch, if necessary—of those holes at either end of this structure. And when we get back to Vesta, I want you to tell me the caliber of the bullet that caused them."

Oreste blinked again. "The caliber of the bullet? You mean

the holes were made by someone firing a gun through...."

"Never mind. Just hop to it. But when you're outside, don't hop too far. We're leaving in half an hour and I don't want to waste time by having to scoot out to retrieve you."

Actually, they were done in twenty minutes.

"Leave all systems functioning," ordered Dooley. "We may have to come back and I don't want to have to go to the trouble of acclimatizing again. Besides," he added, "the cost won't be charged to our department."

The "deceased" was bagged and placed aboard their shuttle, the *S.S. Christie*, and they, the living and the dead, departed the asteroid, which bore the rather romantic name of Albion, at 1:42 hours. It had been a long day for the entire group, especially so for Dooley who had put in a double shift before he was informed that an anxious call from Neal's wife had reached the Station and that Neal couldn't be contacted by radio.

He may have slept a little—*must* have slept a little, because the trip was over, or almost over, with a suspicious suddenness: Vesta was already visible to the naked eye through the so-called window. A glance at his watch showed him that it was now 2:59—the trip out to Albion had been about ten minutes shorter because of the speed differential between the two planetoids. He sat for a minute or two staring at Vesta, which had the apparent size and nondescript shape of a silver nugget, and then said to Phelps, who was sitting, or reclining, next to him, "I've been thinking...."

"Yes, I saw that you were."

"...that if we don't solve this case in five days, I lose my leave of absence."

Phelps shook his head. "Three days. Albion will be moving into Eohippus's sphere of influence in another 84.2 hours. That means the case will come under Russian Jurisdiction if it isn't cleared up before then."

Dooley said, "My God, you're right! We'd be bound over to serve as witnesses and technical experts in the Russian judicial hearings, and I know from experience that those can drag on for months." He was silent a moment, then asked, "How well did you know Carl Neal?"

"I knew him pretty well back in the days when we were both assistants to congressmen in Washington. That was twenty years ago. I've only seen him once since then, when he came out here about three months ago and made a courtesy call at Vesta."

"What sort of man was he?"

"Well, when I knew him he was young, handsome, athletic and very popular with the ladies—he was a bachelor in those days. He had a bit of money, too. He was only working as a congressman's assistant to further his own political career. He was a great guy to be around because he was so full of fun."

"Hummph!" said Dooley. He added, more intelligibly, "Then, you wouldn't say he was a loner?"

"I certainly would not! Most convivial fellow I've met in my life."

"When you saw him at Vesta Station, did he perhaps say he was going to write a novel?"

"Write a novel?" Phelps laughed at the absurdity of the notion. "Carl Neal never *read* a novel in his entire life! I doubt if he ever opened a book of any kind once he got out of college."

"I see. And would you say he was particularly dedicated?"

"To what?"

"To the easing of American/Russian tensions in the Asteroid Belt, for instance?"

"No, I don't think so.... Oh! I see what you're getting at!"

"Yes," said Dooley. "What was a man like that—fairly rich, fairly young, rather ambitious and very gregarious—doing out here in the lonely and thankless role of UN Observer? Clinging by his fingernails to a rock in the middle of the Big Nowhere? Going for weeks or even months without seeing another human face? There's not all that much cash involved—the job only pays starvation wages, about $150,000 a year—and not much credit either: who's impressed by someone's having been a UN Observer in the Belt? No one. And that means your theory about the murder is not likely to be right."

Phelps was astonished. "*My* theory?" The face he turned towards Dooley was so intensely bland it was itself an act of assertion. "That's a little presumptuous of you, isn't it, Tom? To attribute a theory to me when I haven't breathed a word about one?"

"Oh, I suppose so. But your theory, if you did take the trouble to develop one, would be somewhat along these lines, wouldn't it? That your friend Neal was killed by whomever he was playing cards with. That they had an argument over who was winning, or there was some accusation of cheating. That, since there are no signs of struggle inside the igloo, one must have lured the other outside. That they had a fight. That Neal's opponent somehow managed to wrest the helmet off Neal's suit, perhaps fling it away into space—which would be easy enough to do, Albion's gravity being about 2% Earthnorm. He then lost his head, dragged Neal back into the igloo, got him out of his spacesuit and onto the cot and fired a bullet through the igloo to make it look as if Neal had died from one of the natural hazards of life out here...forgetting in his panic that the absence of a helmet was a dead giveaway that murder had been done."

Phelps admitted ruefully, but with a touch of admiration, "That was exactly my theory. What's wrong with it?"

"Mostly, that it's very difficult to remove the helmet of someone's spacesuit without his full cooperation. And that's especially true with the Westinghouse. All suits have built-in safety features to prevent the helmet's being accidentally detached; with the Westinghouse, the wearer has to clench his left hand tightly into a fist and undo the seals at the base of his helmet with his right hand. It takes about twenty seconds. Think how difficult that would make it for an attacker, especially a single attacker, to forcibly remove the helmet. No, what we have here is not a second degree murder—an explosion of anger, an argument over cards that got out of hand—but a murder coldly planned in advance."

"I'm afraid I don't quite see that."

"Consider. A man like Neal wouldn't be out here, in a position like that, unless he had something else going for him. Something big."

"But...what could that be?"

"Spying."

"You mean...like in one of those creaky old spy movies of the Cold War of the nineteenth—or is it the twentieth?—century, where one side steals the other's secrets to keep it from blowing up the world?"

For some reason Dooley was irritated by the question. Or perhaps he was annoyed by the smirk that accompanied it. "Ralph, there's more than one kind of spying! What I had in mind was something a little less glamorous than military or scientific espionage. Industrial spying. The Russians have been making a profit out of mining the asteroids for the last thirty years: just marginal profits, but still profits, whereas it's been a losing proposition with us. There's even been some talk of our abandoning the Belt entirely, which would mean simply handing the world market for minerals over to the Russians. That would be a blow to our national pride, and, of course, there are billions of dollars and rubles at stake. Perhaps Neal was sent out here to find out how the Russkies are doing it. And, if that's so, it means his murder has international implications...and I don't much like that."

Phelps's admiration was ungrudging now. "You know, I've been talking for the last two or three years of doing a book about you, and I'm going to do it too! Someday. I'll be your... what is it? Boswell?"

"Watson, I think you mean."

"Watson. But there are problems," said Phelps, shaking his head gravely. "Artistic problems. I want to include two or three of your cases, like the Schleffin sabotage and the kidnapping of the Russian consul, as I think a single case wouldn't give enough material for an impressive book. But I don't want an episodic book, either. I want something that's artistically coherent and I just don't see as yet how I can tie them all together thematically."

"Well, keep trying," said Dooley, with an ironic sideways look. He was more than a little ashamed of the pleasurable jolt the notion of such a book gave his vanity.

CHAPTER THREE

Vesta now filled the window. Off to one side of it was the space-cup towards which they were dropping with alarming speed. As always, Dooley was unable to repress a touch of panic fear: he braced his right foot hard against the floor, as if he were putting on the brakes of a ground-car. But they weren't smashed to bits this time, either. Again, as always, they were caught firmly within the magnetic/gravitic field of the cup, and the cup and ship together went whirling in slowing, tightening circles around Vesta. On the first go-around Dooley saw the heavy face of Hap Lyles, the gravitic engineer, peering out of an observation port in the rock, and on the second something far more unusual: a large ship touching the underside of the asteroid like a baby whale snuggling against its mother. It wasn't until the fourth or fifth go-around that he saw the Red Star emblazoned on the side of the ship.

The *S.S. Christie* came to a rest at Lock #3. Its crew had barely gotten inside the rock and out of their spacesuits when they heard a familiar voice speaking from the wall-annunciators: "Inspector Dooley and Commissioner Phelps, report to Commissioner Watt's office immediately."

The two looked at each other in disgust, and Dooley said, "Why can't the bastard let us get some sleep first?"

Despite this grumbling, they presented themselves at the door of Watt's office some two minutes later.

"Sit down, gentlemen," said Watt, with guarded courtesy. He was barely middle-aged, not yet seventy, but with a heavy-set body and jowly face. His complexion was florid, and veins stood out on his forehead and temples—he alarmed some people by seeming to be on the verge of a stroke, but others suspected that his collar was simply too tight. He was the only man inboard Vesta to wear a suit and tie; everyone else was wearing khaki shirts and shorts (as were Phelps and Dooley at the moment), laboratory smocks, or comfortable leotards.

Watt repeated, "Sit down!" and waved a heavy hand. They lowered themselves into the two chairs in front of the desk and eyed the man behind it with no very great liking. Dooley had reason enough to remember Watt's disrespectful treatment of him in the past and there was between Watt and Phelps a kind of rivalry, although it was not one the good-natured Phelps had sought. He, Phelps, was responsible for seeing that government regulations and laws were observed by the companies mining the Belt. His authority extended throughout the entire American Sector—except inside Vesta where, for complicated administrative reasons (perfectly sensible, once they were understood) Watt reigned supreme. This wouldn't have bothered Phelps at all, if it weren't that Watt constantly went out of his way to remind him of his subordinate position. His attitude seemed to be, "You may be a Big Shot outside this rock, but, by God, you're not going to lord it over me!"—although no man born of woman was ever less likely to lord it over anyone than was Ralph Phelps.

"Now," said Watt, "will you, Chief Inspector Thomas Dooley, Head of the Security-Forces stationed on Vesta, Asteroid Belt, American Sector"—Dooley smiled at the pedantry of this address, but surmised that Watt was recording the conversation for future reference—"will you please tell us exactly what it was you found on Albion?"

Dooley did so, in plain, concise language. He finished: "I conclude that United Nations Observer Carl Neal was murdered by person or persons unknown, for reasons unknown."

Commissioner Watt regarded him with a slight smile, but made no comment. The smile held and the silence held...and held, for perhaps a whole minute. Dooley and Phelps glanced at each other in puzzlement.

And then a scathing voice sounded in the room:

"Brilliant!"

There was so much scorn and contempt packed into that one word that it was like a splash of acid. Phelps flinched.

"You're a regular Sherlock Holmes of the Asteroid Belt, aren't you?" The voice was coming from the speaker of the telephone on Watt's desk. "You should be the hero of a television series."

Watt said, "Mrs. Neal," using a form of address made fashionable by the Vintage movement....

And Phelps murmured, "You mean—that's a *woman's* voice?"

"...I very much regret your husband's untimely death and I assure you the entire resources of this Station will be concentrated on bringing the perpetrator to justice."

Dooley was puzzled. "Mrs. Neal, where are you? You can't be on Mars."

There would of course be another minute before that question could be answered, but Watt interposed with some information:

"She left Marstation four days ago in a privately-owned ship, the *Rendell*. She's now thirty light-seconds away. She'll be here tomorrow at 16:24 hours."

The scalding voice came again:

"Do you bastards realize that this conversation is costing me a *hundred dollars a second*? And you're wasting my time with *small-talk*!"

Dooley said, "Mrs. Neal, there's no need to talk at all. You will be here in a few hours. I'll give you all the details then. Goodnight. I'm much overdue for bed."

He started to heave himself up from the chair—thanks to Hap Lyles, he enjoyed about one half his Earthside weight on Vesta—but was waved back down by Watt.

The seconds ticked away, sixty of them, and then there was an explosion of expletives, ending with:

"Who does this flunky think he is? He can't talk to me like

that, just because he has a title and is wearing some ridiculous uniform. I'll have his job...."

"You wouldn't want my job," muttered Dooley.

"...and see that he's sent back to Earth."

"Yes—*please!*"

Watt raised a hand to caution Dooley against speaking. "Mrs. Neal, the administration of this Station intends you no discourtesy whatsoever. I will speak to the Chief Inspector," with a wink at Dooley, "about his tone to you. But, as you say, this conversation is costing you a great deal of money and you *will* be here in just a few hours. My profound regrets and apologies, Mrs. Neal. I look forward to meeting you again."

Another wait, perhaps a microsecond shorter this time. "I'll bet you do! But don't get your hopes up!"

Watt leaned quickly forward and touched one of the ivory studs at the right side of his desk. Even this exertion, small as it was, had the effect of deepening the color of his face.

Dooley said, "You know the woman?"

"Oh, yes. I knew her years ago, long before she married Neal."

And Dooley noticed an intonation suspiciously like self-congratulation.

"A difficult woman, I would say," said Phelps. "She seems to have an exaggerated sense of her own importance."

Watt shook his head. "It's not all that exaggerated. She's a close friend of the President and also a close friend," with a wink at the two of them, "of Senator Bailey."

"Bailey...," mused Dooley. "Isn't that the senator who appointed you?"

Watt's hand, which he had carelessly left lying on the desk by the row of ivory studs, twitched irritably.

It was Phelps who replied, "It is. I knew him slightly myself about fifteen years ago, when he was involved in a scandal with the underaged daughter of President Markley...."

"Never mind!" snapped Watt, his hand twitching like a dead spider that's been galvanized. "That's ancient history. Besides, there was nothing to it. The charges were dismissed. It was all a misunderstanding. Senator Bailey is a fine man." He turned to Dooley. "Now look here, Chief Inspector, I know you feel for me that contemptuous distrust a career civil servant always feels for a political appointee...."

"No such thing," said Dooley. "I'm not quite that simple-minded."

"And *I*," said Phelps, "am a political appointee."

"...but I *have* been appointed and I am responsible for the management of this entire Station and everything connected with it, including this murder investigation. I am very grateful to Senator Bailey, but it can't matter to you who appointed me. What does matter is this: his committee has peremptory power over this Station and the American Sector of the Belt. He can terminate the careers of all or any of us, including you and Commissioner Phelps, if he thinks we're bungling this investigation. So I suggest you don't bungle it."

Dooley laughed. "I won't have much chance to bungle it. I'm leaving for Earth in five days time."

"If the investigation is completed, successfully, you will. Otherwise, you won't."

"Just a minute, Commissioner Watt," said Dooley, with a razor-thin edge to his voice. "The Regulations state that no one is to be employed in the Belt for a period longer than two years without a three month break. You know that...."

"I should: you've mentioned it often enough."

"...and you also know that I have been here for five years without Earthside leave. That is contrary to policy...."

"Policy can be set aside in case of emergency, and there have been many emergencies. The miners' strike, the Schleffin sabotage, the power outage...."

"...and I intend to take my Christmas leave, whether this case is settled or not."

"You will do no such thing, Chief Inspector! If you leave this Station without my permission, I can have you discharged for gross insubordination. And that means your pension would be suspended...indefinitely, if need be. Now, Mrs. Neal is going to be here in just a few hours and you're going to need all your wits about you in dealing with her, so I suggest you get some sleep. Go to bed."

Dooley felt his face growing warm and knew it was probably as red as Watt's—but he controlled himself and rose from his chair with as much dignity as his rage and the low gravity would permit. Phelps followed his example.

Dooley looked back from the door. Watt studied his face.

"Goodnight, Commissioner," said Dooley. Watt, smiling slightly, nodded his head. "And," added Dooley, "goodnight to you too, Senator Bailey."

Watt's right hand did a double-take. His slight smile faded. He stared. They both stared at each other...for perhaps thirty seconds before a voice, resonant, smooth, urbane, sliding on chuckles, sounded in the room:

"A cold shot, Inspector: Evidently, the stories I've hear about you are true. I look forward to meeting you someday."

"My guess is that you will," said Dooley, as he and Phelps turned to leave.

CHAPTER FOUR

Although he had gone to bed at 4 A.M., Vesta Time, which was also New York Time, Chief Inspector Thomas Dooley opened his eyes promptly at seven, as he always did, when a single, tactful note chimed beside his pillow. The bed in which he found himself was small, not large enough for two persons (something of which he was at times regretfully aware) and the room was small, although almost luxurious by Station standards. He had a carpet, an easy chair—stuffed, not blow-up—an imitation-wood table and matching chair, a bedside table and video console, a clothes closet, a water-closet, and a cabinet that held his prized collection of 242 spools of mid-twentieth century American films: prized in secret because he had an unexamined feeling that the fascination he felt for such antique movies was a kind of weakness; and so no one else knew about the collection, not even Ralph Phelps.

He flung back the covers with a sigh and sat on the side of the bed for a while, thinking, or perhaps brooding, over the case. He sat for ten minutes as motionless as Rodin's The Thinker, but with both hands on his knees; abruptly came to life, leaned forward and punched a single button on his bedside table.

"Oreste?"

"I'm here, Chief." (Oreste was always there.) "There are two things I'd like you to do this morning—in addition, you understand, to checking the caliber of that bullet and the fingerprints on the cards. First, I want to know the meaning of that scribble on Neal's table. Show it to Heloise. She'll come up with something. She always does."

"Okay. And?"

"You remember that half-collapsed chair which Cyril photographed from all angles? Ask Ito to take that tape to the Lab and have them tell us under what atmospheric pressure that chair would be inflated to full size."

There was a silence of perhaps ten seconds before Oreste said,

"Well, I guess that's why you're the Chief Inspector and I'm a flunky."

Dooley allowed himself (since he knew his subordinate couldn't see it) a smile that was almost affectionate. "Oreste, do you know what the two greatest vices in the world are? I'll give you a hint. The first is impatience."

"And the second?"

"Impatience."

The pause this time lasted only five seconds. "Well...I suppose you won't need all this information until, say, Friday?"

"Friday, hell! I want it *today*, if not sooner!"

He punched a button, disconnecting Oreste, then punched four others.

"Hap? Tom. There's a Russian ship tethered at...Dock 7, I guess it is. What can you tell me about it?"

"The *S.S. Raskolnikov*. Three thousand tons. Fully automated. One man crew: Petra Wetjen. Destination: Ganymede. Loading supplies purchased through UNI, chiefly materials of interest to the Ganymedans. Wetjen has no valid U. S. passport and so can't come inboard Vesta; he's confined to the ship."

"Beautiful. Now, is it possible there's another ship in our vicinity? Say about fifteen light-seconds out?"

"Now, how in hell did you know that! You're right. There's a ship sixteen light-seconds away. Its radar profile is identical with that of the *Raskolnikov*. Probably a sister-ship, built in the DaNang shipyards. So far it hasn't responded to radio. Its trajectory takes it close to Albion, Vesta and Eohippus. We won't know which one it's headed for until it starts decelerating, which it'd better do soon, if it's coming to us. It'll have to match our speed exactly, since it's too big for the space-cup to handle."

"Nothing else?"

"No...not yet."

"Thanks, Hap."

Dooley skipped breakfast because he had an errand to run. He met Phelps and the two took one of the shuttles to Pebbleton, a small (and growing ever smaller, because of the mining) asteroid, to take care of some paperwork lingering from the Schleffin affair. They had to make another attempt to obtain depositions from three mining engineers who were reluctant to give them. Dooley thought he might have to try a little brow-beating, something he never relished doing. But when he and Phelps arrived, they found that the resistance had unexpectedly collapsed. The engineers had at last understood that, despite the enormity of what had happened, they were in no danger of incriminating themselves and gave their testimonies cheerfully. The two were back at Vesta by noon.

Phelps went to his office, where he had an administrative assistant and a nondescript helper, and Dooley went to meet Oreste for lunch in what was officially termed the Refectory, although everyone called it the Cafeteria. The videomurals in the large room showed idealized Earthside scenes: this week it was coconut trees, bamboo huts, a large expanse of sand and an even larger expanse of busy water. He and Oreste took their usual table in the far left corner, with surf breaking on the beach and washing—the illusion was perfect—to within a dozen feet of where they sat. They hadn't sat very long before they were joined by Heloise Jamison, the archivist. She was a slim, trim, good-looking brunette, thirty at the most, who, in addition to her contracted duties, worked as a stringer for the Interplanetary News Service and published a weekly newsletter for the denizens of the Station. She habitually joined them for lunch and sometimes for other meals as well, there being a kind of pretence that she was interested in Dooley, although everyone knew that she was really interested in Oreste...except, possibly,

Oreste himself.

After Dooley had amply sampled his ham and eggs, he said, *apropos* of nothing while draining a cup of coffee,

"Ganymede?"

"Ganymede," replied Oreste. He added, after a pause, "Well, I guess that's why...."

"Never mind!" said Dooley. He didn't want to see Oreste downplay himself before Heloise. "The fingerprints?"

"Neal's. His only. The party playing cards with him was wearing gloves, it seems."

"He was probably still in his spacesuit. We didn't leave any fingerprints, either, when we were poking around the igloo. The bullet?"

Oreste chuckled. "It came from what's called a .45 caliber gun. A relic from the glorious past, like in one of those creaky old gangster movies." Dooley, the collector of antique movies, felt a twinge of annoyance. "When I was at the Police Academy, we had some handguns in our museum, but I haven't seen one since."

Dooley said, "There are still a few around. I wouldn't be surprised to learn that there was one or two at this very Station." He didn't add that *he* had a .45 in one of the drawers of his dresser. He turned to Heloise. "That scribble was in Russian, of course."

"Of course. The English translation is: 'The Vault of Memory.'"

Dooley repeated the phrase to himself. "Sounds like it might be a scrap of poetry."

"Yes. Or the title of a poem. Pushkin, maybe. I don't know: our computer is unable to identify it. We'll have to get help from Earthside archives."

"You've wired INS about Neal's murder?"

"Oh, sure—the moment your Lieutenant here whispered it into my shell-like ear. It means a fat little check for me, you know?"

"I have a question to ask about the Pugs?"

She made a comical little *moue* of disapproval. "People of good will don't call them Pugs. That would be like calling your friend Ito a Wog."

"Okay: Ganymedans, then."

"I'm not sure I can tell you anything you don't already know. They were discovered just thirty years ago and, so far, they're the only other intelligent creatures we human beings have ever run across. They live on Ganymede, Jupiter's largest moon, and thrive on a noxious mixture of ammonia and methane and such like. They have a rather primitive culture. They don't wear clothes or live in cities, but they do build houses and roads and raise crops. Curiously enough, they have a kind of technology, but it's all gears and levers—no electricity."

Oreste asked, "Why are they called Pugs?"

But Dooley, who had listened with some impatience to Heloise's recitation, interrupted. "All I wanted to know is this: isn't there some guy who's lived with the Pu—with the Ganymedans for years and is supposed to be *the* authority on them?"

"Yes. A Russian. I've forgotten his name."

"Petra Wetjen?"

"That's right."

Phelps appeared suddenly, as if he had risen from the surf. He pulled out a chair and sat down, his back to the crashing waves. "Hey, one mystery's solved, at least."

"Which one is that?"

"The mystery of why a man like Carl Neal would choose to live all alone on an asteroid out in the middle of The Big Nowhere, as Tom here calls it. If I was married to a woman like that, I'd do it too."

"Perhaps you have?" hinted Heloise with a sly smile.

"Nothing like it! I'm a lifelong bachelor, my dear. And, besides, Vesta," looking around fondly at the seemingly spacious scene, the slightly-waving palm trees, the whispering surf, "is a paradise compared to that rock Neal was camping on. Still, I don't blame him." He shuddered. "Brrr! What a shrew!"

Dooley glanced at his watch. "She's going to be here in less than five hours. I'm supposed to be there to meet her when she comes...eyeball to eyeball, I suppose. Perhaps you two guys," meaning Phelps and Oreste, "should be there to back me up. That's an order in your case, Oreste."

Heloise laughed. "As Editor, Star Reporter and everything else of *The Vestal Virgin*"—her pet name for the newsletter, otherwise known as *The Rockland Review*—"I'll be there too."

CHAPTER FIVE

Waiting in the terminal lobby, they heard the impact of Mrs. Neal's vehicle being docked. The shock went through the solid rock of the Station like an anticipatory shudder; sounding for all the world as if contact had been made just on the other side of the outward-facing wall. They all turned towards the door in that wall: Dooley, Phelps, Oreste, Heloise and a crowd of some thirty other persons who somehow had heard about the expected arrival and had wandered in. The population of Vesta was so small (512, give or take a few miners who were always coming and going on the shuttles) that any visitor was an event.

"Well," said Oreste after a while, "what's keeping her?"

"Patience!" advised a voice from the rear—the voice of Commissioner Watt, who had just entered the room. He seemed to be in unusually good spirits, the eyes in his florid face playfully alive. "She inboarded at Lock #4 a mile off, so it'll take a minute or so for her to get here on the minirail."

The door opened at that very moment and a woman entered the room. She was closely followed by Hap Lyles, familiar to everyone there as the gravitics engineer, but a good while passed before anyone even noticed his presence.

For all eyes were fastened—riveted—on the woman, who stood looking them over with a faint smile. Dooley stared too, for she was the most beautiful woman he had ever seen. And he knew (for he was in the habit of unflinchingly facing facts) that she was the most beautiful woman anyone had ever seen. Her hair was red (of course) and fell in carefully crafted waves and ringlets to her shoulders. Her eyes were green and her pale creamy skin was untouched by even the slightest blemish. It seemed to him that she was wearing absolutely no makeup—he may have been mistaken about that; but, makeup or no, she was the most beautiful woman he had ever seen. Her features were saved from classic perfection by a slightly snub nose—saved just in the nick of time, as it seemed to him. Perfection might have chilled her beauty a little and made it bearable, but, as it was, that nose gave her face an almost unbearable poignancy: for it made it adorable as well as beautiful...and she was, quite simply, the most beautiful woman he had ever seen.

And her beauty was not confined to her face—not by any means. As it happened, she was wearing a skintight leotard, but many women, perhaps most women, on Vesta, wore leotards. Familiarity had created a climate of casual acceptance and no woman could render herself more desirable by putting on such a commonplace dress—but this woman transfigured the commonplace. Her body, as displayed in that swirling pattern of black and silver zebra stripes, was perfection itself. It was full without being grossly so. Another inch here, or an inch there, and the onlooker might have smiled as at something slightly grotesque or comical or lewdly suggestive and her dignity as a person compromised; but, as it was, her figure was beyond reproach. It was (Dooley repeated the phrase) perfection itself. He was conscious of a vague physical discomfort and restlessness, and of something else too: a pang or throb that was like the residue of some old forgotten grief to which he could put no name.

He was the first to break the spell. He looked around and saw that everyone in the room was staring, except two middle-aged women near the door who had averted their eyes. Oreste was pale, the freckles across the bridge of his nose unusually prominent and well-defined. Heloise was staring, her lips parted. Hap Lyles' jaw had dropped so far that one might have thought he had somehow succeeded in increasing the gravitational attraction in its immediate vicinity to some three or four times

Earthnorm. And yet...and yet, Dooley reflected, this was the woman with that scalding, scathing voice! He turned towards Phelps to share with him his amused awareness of this fact... and saw that his friend was ludicrously shaken, his mouth wide open as if in imitation of Hap's. Only Commissioner Watt's mouth was closed and that rather smugly; there was even, to Dooley's disgust, a touch of the Mona Lisa about it.

Watt now stepped forward out of the crowd and extended his hand. "Welcome to Vesta, Mrs. Neal.... I would offer you the key to the Station, if we had one."

Her lips parted...and Dooley expected to hear her say something like, "You can keep your key in your pants!" in the grating voice that had issued from the speaker in Watt's office; but, instead, what he heard was a voice of thrilling sweetness, in which she assured Dear Joseph, as she called him, of her great happiness in seeing him again.

"It was so *very* kind of you to welcome me personally. I know how very busy you must be. And," looking around, "such a warm welcome, from so *many* people. It makes me feel quite important. I'm sure," she said, addressing everyone generally, "that I'll get to know you all, and call you all my friends, before I go." Oreste was standing in his khaki shirt and shorts at the front of the crowd. She stepped towards him, touched his hand. "You must be Chief Inspector Dooley. So unexpectedly young! And so very handsome!"

Oreste managed to say, "No, this is Chief Inspector Dooley," but she couldn't have found that very helpful, since he didn't remove his eyes from her face or his hand from hers. But she understood him. She looked around, saw Dooley standing a half dozen feet away and moved towards him.

"Of course! I should have known! The famous Inspector Dooley...."

Famous? He wondered about that.

"...could only be a man of maturity and experience." She placed her very soft hand—he was astonished by its softness— in his clumsy and calloused paw and looked up into his face. "I see now that the investigation of my beloved husband's death is in safe hands. Those unflinching eyes, that grim mouth, that terrible chin! That chin alone promises swift and terrible retribution to all wrong-doers."

The words suggested mockery, but the pathetic appeal in her voice and in those wonderful eyes made him want to reject any such suggestion as a palpable and outrageous absurdity.

He said, "I hope you had a nice trip, Mrs. Neal."

"Oh, no! I was beside myself with grief and anxiety the whole time."

He had good reason not to believe that and yet he heard himself saying, "I'm sorry. Awfully stupid of me to say such a thing."

"You're forgiven. And I apologize for my tone of last night. I was awfully upset. I hope you understand that?"

"Oh, yes." He could feel himself sliding into graciousness again, and to preserve his self-respect, he added, "Murder upsets everyone."

She gave him a quick look and withdrew her hand—he felt the deprivation. She said, "I don't believe my husband was murdered."

"Why not?"

"Because no one could possibly hate Carl. He was the sweetest, most loveable man who ever lived."

"Perhaps so, but, you know, Mrs. Neal, there are people in the world who are *not* sweet and loveable and they sometimes kill those who are."

She moved away a few steps. "Not Carl. No, not Carl. Never!" She somehow produced a handkerchief—to his amazement, because he didn't see where she could possibly have secreted it—and touched her eyes with it. "We all loved him and he'll always have a special place in our memory."

Dooley was reminded of "The Vault of Memory." She looked around at him—"What?"—and he realized that he must have murmured the phrase aloud.

"Oh, nothing. A scrap of poetry. Mrs. Neal, this may be

painful to you, but perhaps the least cruel thing I can do is to put your doubts to rest. There can be no doubt that your husband was murdered. The helmet of his spacesuit was missing. It wasn't inside the igloo, and he couldn't possibly have come in from outside without it."

"So you said last night in your report. But isn't it possible that you just overlooked it? After all, you must have been in a terrible hurry."

He shook his head. "We weren't in too much of a hurry to videotape every cubic inch inside the igloo. We couldn't possibly have missed the helmet."

And she wasn't too grief-stricken to be amused by his tone of absolute certainty. "The purloined helmet," she murmured. "Still, I can't believe it. Carl had no enemies."

"In that case," said Dooley, "he must have been murdered by one of his friends. What friends did he have, Mrs. Neal?"

Commissioner Watt stepped between them. "Chief Inspector Dooley, I will not allow you to badger Mrs. Neal at this moment."

"I have no intention of badgering her! As for the moment, I'll gladly repeat my questions at any time she thinks appropriate."

She said, "That's all right, Joseph. I don't feel in the least badgered and I'm sure the Inspector doesn't mean to torment me so." She dabbed at her eyes with the handkerchief again. "Carl had so many friends. He knew everyone and was liked by everyone. He had friends all over Earth. He had friends at Mars Station and out here in the Asteroid Belt. Why, he even had friends," she said, "in the Russian Sector."

"Can you name one?"

"Oh...." Turning away a little, her face prettily clouded by the effort of memory. "Petra Wetjen."

"Wetjen? Now, that's convenient! I can easily question him about his friendship with your husband. He's here now."

She had started to move away from him, but this stopped her. She looked around at him with a slow-forming, incredulous smile. Her eyes slipped past him, searched the crowd.

"You must mean," said Watt—and Dooley noticed that the

Commissioner's face was even more flushed than it usually was; "you must mean the operator of that Russian ship docked at Port 7—I'm afraid you can't question him, Dooley. He has no visa and so can't set foot inside Vesta. And you can't go inboard his ship because of the quarantine."

"Quarantine? This isn't 1945. Advances in medical science have done away with quarantines."

"Not in this case. He and his ship have been down among the Pugs on Ganymede and who knows what alien microorganisms he may have picked up...."

"In that case, I'll have to talk to him by radio."

The Commissioner sighed. "Okay, you've got me there. But if he chooses not to answer, there's nothing you can do about it. But enough of this! Edith—I mean Mrs. Neal—has been cramped inside that small flyer for days and must be exhausted."

"Yes, I am *so* tired," said Edith Neal. She placed the back of one hand against her forehead, and, with her eyes half closed, swayed, as if with extreme exhaustion. There was an answering movement in the crowd, as every male in it leaned forward, instinctively yearning to snatch her up and carry her away to some place where she could rest comfortably.

But Commissioner Watt had the prior claim. "Clear the way!" he shouted, waving an arm majestically, like Moses parting the Red Sea. "Clear the way! This is Edith Markley Neal, the daughter of a president!"

The crowd obediently parted and he led Edith Markley Neal through it and out the door. The crowd closed behind them and streamed away after them.

* * * * * * *

The four friends—Dooley, Phelps, Heloise, and Oreste— followed at a more leisurely pace, back down the featureless corridor that led to the general living quarters of Vesta.

Phelps said in a marveling voice, "Neal must have been insane! Imagine deserting a woman like that! What could have lured him out here, so far away from her?"

"Yes," muttered Dooley. "*What?*"

Heloise had taken Dooley's arm as they walked; a habit of hers. "You know, it's the damnedest thing—I don't feel the slightest jealousy of her. She's so completely out of my league, there just wouldn't be any point in it." She laughed with wonderment. "That woman is from another planet!"

Dooley's casual eye sought out Oreste, who was lagging a step or two behind the group. For a fear had suggested itself to him: that, after seeing that Goddess, his young man might never again be interested in any mere mortal woman such as Heloise. He saw that Oreste's eye was resting on Heloise, but perhaps without really seeing her...for it wasn't an observing eye but a dreaming one. Dooley looked away.

CHAPTER SIX

An Indiana childhood. Snow on the ground and he still playing with his sled, even though it is after dark; the glowing windows of a two-story farmhouse in the near distance. His mother appears in the lighted doorway and calls him into supper.

"Aw, Ma, not yet!" but she turns and vanishes back into the house. He looks around, reluctant to go into supper and to bed. Standing all about him are trees with bare limbs, stark in their beauty; and, looking up past and through the limbs, he sees the stars in the sky.

And then a dreadful thing: he sees the stars slip and fall from their places, smear across the sky as streaks of light. Some of the streaks are very broad and bright. One coming from the northeastern section of the sky grows and grows until it is a band of flame many yards across. It moves towards him with a terrible silence, and yet he seems to sense, lagging far behind, a trembling vibration like that of an on-coming freight train. And he knows where that river of fire will touch ground...and in the instant that he knows he sees it touch, sees the farmhouse explode with a great outward-reaching gush of light, noise and heat that lifts him from his feet, so that he falls backward upon his sled....

...and lay there, not on the sled but on a comfortable bed in the dark. It was some time before he fully knew that he wasn't lying in bed in the old Indiana farmhouse but in a narrow cot in a windowless chamber inside the stony heart of Vesta.

He lay quietly, steeped in darkness, for some minutes more,

then uttered a grunt of alarm. He threw back the covers, got out of bed and thumbed a single button on his communicator. A sleepy voice answered.

Dooley said, "Sergeant Ito, I know it's late...."

"Early, I think you mean."

"...but this may be important. Those tapes we made in Neal's igloo—where are they now? Still in the Physical Sciences area?"

There was a yawning pause, as if Ito were some light-seconds from Vesta, although his apartment was actually no more than a hundred yards from Dooley's. Then,

"No. I picked them up just before going to bed. Four or five hours ago. They're in the secured area in our Department.

"Meet me there in ten minutes."

Dooley wrapped a robe around himself and left his cell. He walked down a dismal hallway to an uninviting door, opened it and stepped into and walked down what seemed to be a dark country lane. It might have been a continuation of his dream, except that he was now moving through a warm summer night. Crickets hushed their noise as he passed. The light of a full moon was reflected dully from the pale trunks of sycamores, and between the trunks he caught the glimmer of candlelight from distant windows. He could hear from somewhere to his left the murmur of moving water (the Wabash, he supposed) and he heard from far away the lonely wail of a locomotive, a sound so eerily appealing that it stopped him in his tracks... though only for a moment. He went on, and found Ito waiting for him before and beneath the large oak that masked the door of the Security Forces office. Ito had found time to completely and neatly dress, even putting on his usual pair of dark-rimmed "glasses"—an affectation common to those proud of a Japanese heritage.

It took them three minutes to retrieve the two tapes from an inner office and another ten minutes to run them from beginning to end.

Not that there was all that much to see.

Ito was pale with shock. "Erased," he whispered. "Both tapes completely erased!" He turned his lensless spectacles on Dooley. "This is scary. It means some outsider has gained access to our security area."

Dooley said, "Maybe; maybe not. It probably wasn't done here, if that's any comfort to you. It was probably done in the Physical Sciences Department, to which almost anyone can gain access. A lot of people must have known the tapes were there and pretty much what was on them. It's awfully hard to keep a secret in a place like this, especially when you're working with volunteers who aren't sworn to secrecy. And that's another thing," he added, laying a hand on Ito's shoulder, "I think It best if whoever did this doesn't know that we've already discovered it. Don't mention it to anyone. And I mean, *anyone*."

Ito's smile was tentative, uneasy. "Not even to Commissioner Watt?"

Dooley didn't reply but stood casually straightening his robe and watching Ito. Then: "Do you suppose you could gain access to Mrs. Neal's flyer?"

Ito turned his dark-ringed eyes on him again. "It wouldn't present any mechanical difficulties, If that's what you mean."

"Yes, that's what I mean. Ordinarily, I wouldn't dream of doing such a thing without first obtaining a warrant from Commissioner Watt. But I don't want to trouble him just now. He's undoubtedly still in bed."

Ito's eyes didn't blink. "Did you want me to look for anything in particular?"

Dooley told him, and added, "After that, you can go back to bed. I won't expect you in the office...until, say, nine o'clock."

Ito laughed and left. Dooley went back to his own bachelor apartment, turned out the light, took off his robe and wiggled in between the sheets. He knew he wouldn't be able to sleep, but he experimentally closed his eyes, anyway, and had barely done so, as it seemed, when the note chimed, informing him that it was seven o'clock.

He punched a button and was immediately answered.

"I'm here, Chief."

"Oreste, doesn't anyone else ever call you?"

"Not at seven in the morning."

But Dooley knew that he never got a busy signal when he called the young man, regardless of what time it was, and that seemed to him a little sad.

He told Oreste about the tapes and the lieutenant made a long low whistle expressive of consternation. "That means we'll have to go back and tape everything over again."

"No," said Dooley. "I think we can put this little development to better use than that. It might take some working, though. I'll tell you about it at lunch. See you then."

He was a little slow for once in reaching out to disconnect the line and he heard Oreste say something, very low, which he failed to catch; but before he could say, "What's that?" he heard a soft sweet voice murmuring something in reply...and then the connection was broken at the other end.

He sat for a while looking at the instrument before he touched the disconnect button at his end. He knew that half a dozen women at the Station had "set their caps" for the handsome lieu-tenant...but that certainly wasn't any of his business, was it? But maybe he didn't need to feel so sorry for the guy, after all.

He tapped out a familiar four-digit number on the machine.

"Hap? What's the status of the *S.S. Raskolnikov*?"

"The pilot's inloading the last of his requisitions now. Ammonia, methane, and so on. Marsh gas, I calls it."

"And I would call it 'coals to Newcastle.' But go on."

"The stuff should be inboard and secured by 13:50, so if you're going to question him in the line of duty...."

"Thanks for the suggestion, Hap," said Dooley, with just a touch of coolness: he hadn't forgotten that ludicrously-dropped jaw of last night. "And the twin ship? Any news of that?"

"Yes. We're in communication now. It's the *S.S. Van Dine*. Guess who's aboard?"

"Senator Bailey."

"That's right. And what a ship it is! Tremendous tonnage. Complete insulation against particle-meteorites, electromagnetic disturbances and the whole spectrum of radiation. Helmholtz engines and fabricated gravity—in fact, its instrumentation and field-generators are superior to what we have here. State of the Art. Like the Russkie ship, of course, only this one's a real luxury yacht besides. There's a Captain, stewards, a gourmet chef and waiters, a barber and beautician, a recreation director, a doctor and nurse, and who knows what else?—maybe hot and cold running chambermaids."

"I'm impressed as all get out. But how can anyone afford a ship like that?"

"No one can. No single individual, anyway. The ship is owned by thirty-one senators who clubbed together on a time-sharing basis. And here's what's funny: all thirty-one are Republicans."

Dooley had to think a moment about that. "You mean... because the boat's named after a Democratic president?"

"Right. And, you know, most of those senators have never spent a whole day on her. She's so expensive to move, they can't afford it. Only a really rich guy like Bailey can pick up the tab without turning pale. Quite a guy, that Bailey! I...I understand he knows her well."

"I guess he should. He's been in and out of her a few times."

Hap Lyles said, "I meant Miss Markley."

Dooley couldn't help grinning. "*Mrs. Neal*, isn't it?"

"He's dead and so she's free again...."

"Look, Hap! Whether she's free or not can hardly matter to you and me. She can have her pick of men who are younger and handsomer than both of us put together."

Hap's voice blazed. "Then what in the Hell's she doing with Commissioner Watt! That guy's *older* than both of us! And I can tell you one thing—she didn't spend the night in the apartment assigned to her, and Watt didn't answer his phone last night. I *know*, because I called him at two and three and four on the emergency line. About something that came up."

Dooley said sadly, "Forget it, Hap." And then: "Can you let me know when the *Raskolnikov* leaves? Say fifteen minutes before?"

And Hap replied with too heavy a touch of cheerful friendliness, "Sure can, old buddy!"

* * * * * * *

The phone buzzed just as Dooley reached his office that morning. He knew who it was and said, as he pushed the button,
"Well?"

"It's even better than you thought. You could drink the stuff without feeling any ill-effects."

"Thanks, Ito. You can take the rest of the day off."

"Okay. You know where to find me, if you need me." Ito had a passion for miniature golf and spent most of his free time at the Station's Playland.

Dooley made several attempts during the rest of the morning and most of the afternoon to contact the *Raskolnikov* by telephone, but always with the same result. Although a radio-link had clearly been established, there was no response, no matter how long he let the futile buzzings go on—he felt that he could almost hear the lonely sound they made inside the shell of the giant spaceship. "It seems," he confided to himself, "that Petra Wetjen is 'not at home' to callers."

He sat and waited patiently at his desk, shuffling a few papers. He hadn't had lunch with Oreste, after all, and, in fact, had seen very little of him the whole day: the young man had been kept busy with the small errands and chores that Ito usually performed.

The expected call came through from Hap Lyles at 3:30.

Dooley instantly contacted Oreste and ordered him to get everything ship-shape.

He got up, put on an officious khaki jacket over his khaki shirt and left the office.

CHAPTER SEVEN

The showcase avenue of Vesta was Rockland Boulevard, which more than once had been called the Eleventh Wonder of the World. What distinguished it from all other corridors in the honeycombed rock was that it had a videomural running along both sides *and* the ceiling for its entire length, which was more than a mile. It was, in fact, the wooded lane down which Dooley had taken his nighttime stroll; for the mural showed a continuous rural landscape, so that the illusion (making allowance for the perfect flatness and unvarying width of the ground) was of walking down a back-country lane in late nineteenth century Indiana. Dooley now, having gotten past the stands of sycamore and the disguised door of his own office (which opened to a spoken code), walked by fields of corn and wheat, with a lonely farmhouse here and there in the distance, a few barns and haystacks and now and then a farmer trudging off to his fields with a hoe or scythe over his shoulder. The sun overhead was perceptibly warm, but an occasional tree provided shade and there was a slight breeze, so that the overall effect was very pleasant. It was often said by the residents of Vesta that they owed their sanity to Rockland Boulevard. That was, of course, an exaggeration, but Dooley sometimes wondered if he could have gotten through the last five years without the refreshment of his daily stroll down it.

Actually, he was on his way now to the office of Commissioner Watt. He had barely gotten close enough to make out in the distance the rustic gate which fronted for the door of Watt's office when he saw the man himself coming towards him in company with a short, portly man with a partly bald head. Dooley had good reason to know this man too. He was Izak Gerasimov, the Russian Consul in the Asteroid Belt. Two years ago, he, Dooley, had rescued Gerasimov from almost certain death at the hands of the Purgationists, a gang of kidnappers, extortionists and supposed revolutionaries who at that time were infesting the Russian Sector like gravel-hopping fleas.

Gerasimov was far happier to see Dooley than was Watt—not that that was saying much: for Watt's expression clearly showed that Dooley was the last person he wanted to see.

The Russian called out "My old friend!" and came forward with wide-open arms. "My...what is the word? My life-saver. I am here on a good-will visit and had hoped to see you before I left." They shook hands vigorously; Gerasimov had already learned not to kiss Dooley on the cheeks. Watt loitered some nine or ten feet away. "Are you free? Can you spend some time with me? Or are you working on a case?"

"I'm afraid I'm on a case, Izak. And, as it happens, you can be of some help to me. There's a fellow citizen of yours, Petra Wetjen, whose ship is docked here now."

"Ah, Petra, Petra," intoned Gerasimov, "dear old Petra! He is a giant among men, is Petra, and he has the soul of a poet. Petra," he went on in a whining singsong, as if ecstatic in his contemplation of the many excellences of his countryman and yet with a sly look that Dooley knew well, "has delved deep into the soul of Ganymede and has extracted its flavor and...how shall I say it? bottled it for export. Have you seen the television film he made under the auspices of my government and your National Geographic Society? No, I think not; it hasn't reached here yet. The Russian soul—did you know this?—the Russian soul feels a deep nostalgic love for the Ganymedan soul, for as they are so once were we: a pastoral people living a simple communal existence, a virtuous people innocent of property and wealth and all selfish striving, working together under our great Father Stalin for the common good...."

Dooley suppressed a grin, for he had heard this song and dance before and knew the Consul didn't mean a word of it.

"But tell me," said Gerasimov, "what has Petra done? Surely, he has not infracted any of your multitudinous and unintelligible laws?"

Dooley said, "Maybe; maybe not. He is only a few hundred yards from us as we speak...but I haven't been able to speak *to* him. He doesn't respond to my calls. Can you help me there?"

"I rather think I can," said the Consul. He removed a notebook from an inner coat pocket and wrote a series of numbers on one of its pages. "This is an emergency code that will override any inhibitors in his communication system. Use this number and he *must* answer. Mind you! I have complete faith in Petra Wetjen. That man can do no wrong! But if you must ask questions of him, you may ask them in my name as well as yours."

Commissioner Watt called, "Just a minute!" and glided towards them. His face was mottled and dark, as if he had had a touch too much of the Indiana sun. "Representative Gerasimov, you cannot deal with one of my officers except through me. And you, Chief Inspector Dooley, you should know better! There are channels and proper procedures for these things and you must observe them. I am still the ranking officer on Vesta, and if you want to get in touch with this man, you must see me first. But I see no reason"—he was spluttering a little; Dooley drew back to avoid the spray—"I see no reason why you should get in touch with him at all. Petra Wetjen is an honored citizen of the foreign power with which we share the administration of the Asteroid Belt. He is our guest. And he is the United Nations Ambassador Extraordinaire to the Ganymedan People. He is clearly too important a person to be grilled like a common criminal...."

At that moment there was a deeply resonant chunking noise. A vibration ran through wall, floor and ceiling, profoundly agitating late nineteenth century Indiana, which flickered and wavered, threatening to dissolve.

The Russian diplomat looked around, his poise momentarily gone. "Did a meteorite strike Vesta?"

"I think not," said Dooley. "It's a large ship disconnecting from Port #7. In fact, it's the *Raskolnikov*. Petra Wetjen is leaving."

Watt looked back down the corridor in the direction of Port #7—but he failed to turn his face away quickly enough to conceal the relief that had flooded his features.

Dooley said, "I was on my way to see you, Commissioner, when I met you and the Consul here in the hall. But I'm too late: Wetjen has left. Still, there is *something* I can do. I would like your permission to go in pursuit of him...."

Watt turned an astonished face back towards him.

"...in the *S.S. Doyle*."

Watt was congealed; and, finally, could come up with nothing better than, "The *Doyle*? Why can't you take the *Christie*? It's smaller and cheaper to operate."

"The *Doyle* has grappling and boarding equipment," said Dooley with a straight face, "the *Christie* doesn't. My hope is to overtake the *Raskolnikov* and, if Wetjen refuses communication, to get inside her and ask my questions face to face."

The face before him at the moment was a curious study. Dooley was reminded of a freeze-frame in an old movie. He could almost hear the tiny wheels whirring in the man's skull as he calculated the various risks and possibilities.

"But," stammered Watt, "can you overtake it?"

"I'm not sure I can. Perhaps I can't. After all, the Russian ship has Helmholtz engines five times the size of those of the *Doyle* and it will have at least a two-hour head start. But, still," he added with tremendous gravity, "it's my duty to try. And it shouldn't take me away from my duties here for more than... well, say three or four days at the most."

The sly and sagacious Gerasimov had been looking back and forth between Watt's face and Dooley's. When he spoke again his expression was sober, his tone free of even the slightest trace of irony.

"You have my permission, Chief Inspector Dooley, to contact my fellow-citizen Petra Wetjen in whatever manner necessary.

I know his character and know that only death will place him beyond the pale of honor."

He tore from the notebook the page on which he had written the numbers and handed it to Dooley, who pocketed it.

Dooley now looked to Watt expectantly, as if for explicit permission for a relentless pursuit of the Russian ship. Watt gave it, with a short, sharp nod of his head, as if not trusting himself to speak. But here was something curious: although his lips were tightly compressed and his eyes half-lidded, that whimsical mischievousness of manner that had so recently characterized Gerasimov seemed to have transferred itself, somehow, to him.

"I'm on my way," said Dooley.

But his way took him for the moment farther down Rockland Boulevard, for of course he had to pick up Ralph Phelps before he left. And whom should he meet wandering towards him down this homely country lane but that friend himself. He was glad to see that Ralph had apparently received some very good news: he was smiling broadly and seemed to be in a state of genial good humor and excitement, like a child on Christmas Eve.

Phelps saw Dooley and stopped suddenly, gave him a look that plainly said, "What—*you* here?" He put one hand to his forehead and looked about uncertainly; stared at a scarecrow standing in a field of corn some thirty yards, as it seemed, to his right, but it didn't do much to restore his sense of where he was. Dooley felt a twinge of concern, but Phelps's joy was restrained only for a moment. It burst forth again and carried him towards Dooley, blurting out:

"I've done it! It's an incredible artistic breakthrough! I've solved the problems involved in writing those stories about you!" Dooley was at first amazed and then amused and then, despite himself, flattered and pleased. "I won't have the book made up of separate stories one after the other, after all. That would be too episodic. I'll have three separate stories, yes, but they'll run concurrently, side by side. That'll provide suspense all the way to the end. What was blocking me," he went on, his words stumbling over themselves, "what was holding me up, was I couldn't see how the three stories could be tied together at the end without grossly violating the known facts. But it suddenly struck me a few minutes ago...well, maybe a few hours ago; I've lost track of time...it suddenly struck me that I don't have to tie the stories together. No, I'll take the ancient Chinese as my model. They wrote the first mystery novels, like the famous Judge Dee stories, and they always had three separate story-lines running neck-to-neck and they never knitted them together neatly at the conclusion. Don't you see," he said, taking hold of the lapel of Dooley's jacket, "how this one thought solves everything? What a tremendous release! Now," and he stepped back and rubbed his hands together; "now I don't have to just talk about it, I can actually do it!"

"That's nice, Ralph," said Dooley, trying to keep from laughing. "But there's something I want to tell you." He led Phelps to one side of the hall, close to a rustic fence of weather-beaten wood, as if for greater privacy. He looked about. A half dozen persons were walking, strolling, loitering along the boulevard in both directions, but none gave the two men a second look. Dooley leaned close and said in a husky whisper, "The game's afoot!"

Phelps jerked, stared. "I'm glad you said that!"

"Yes, I thought you might be able to use it. Look, we're going off in another hour after that Russian ship, the *Raskolnikov*. We're taking the *Doyle*, which has grappling and boarding equipment, but...."

But Phelps was shaking his head. "No, no, no! I can't go this time. I can't let this 'first fine careless rapture,' as the poet calls it, slip by me. I have to seize the moment. There are things a man waits for all his life," he said, his eyes wandering off irresolutely and settling on the scarecrow, "and when they come he can't let any consideration deter him. Not even...well, not even disappointing an old friend."

Dooley was touched, for he saw that Phelps was genuinely distressed: there was even a glint of tears in his eyes. Poor, tender-hearted guy! He said, "That's all right, Ralph. Don't let it bother you. I'm going to miss having my Watson along, but I can tell you all about it afterwards."

"Afterwards, yes," said Phelps, looking restlessly back down the corridor in the general direction of his neat little apartment, where, no doubt, his dictascriber was patiently awaiting him. "I'll have to know how things come out, because this—yes, *this* case—is going to be one of the three stories.

"I may give each story a separate title and, if so, I'll call this one 'The Asteroid Murder Case.' The other two will be the story of the Schleffin sabotage, which I'll call 'The Rain of Terror'— that's R-A-I-N. Some terrific effects possible there, you know. And the story of how you were called to the Russian Sector to solve the disappearance of the Ambassador—I'll call that 'The Russ Rockland Express,' because of that wild ride at the end. The book as a whole will have the title, *The Big Nowhere*."

"Yes, yes," said Dooley, laughing and clapping Phelps on the shoulder. "I'm sorry you won't be in on the kill this time, but I'll make do with Oreste. I'm off!"

CHAPTER EIGHT

Despite Dooley's dispatch and determination, it took him and Oreste another hour to clear port in the *S.S. Doyle*.

They "streaked out in the wake of the fleeing *Raskolnikov*," as Dooley supposed Ralph Phelps would put it when he wrote the story, although they were actually a few degrees off the other ship's probable course because of the movement of Vesta along its orbit.

"I guess," said Oreste, with a sly look at his chief, "we shouldn't waste any time before programming the computer for Albion."

Dooley made a grunt expressive of amusement and approval.

"You're coming along, Oreste! One of these days you'll be taking over my job. Perhaps sooner than I think. But let's wait until there are a few chunks of rock between us and the Station before we veer off. That'll be a while yet. We don't want whoever's on radar duty to be able to sort us out from the other debris."

Oreste thought this over, drawing his pale eyebrows towards the freckled bridge of his nose. "You don't mean Hap?"

"Whoever," said Dooley, bending to peer through what he and everyone else called a telescope, although technically it was an "optical enhancer." "We can't take any chances, so we'll just stay on this fellow's tail for a while."

They were moving out towards the lonelier, darker and (as Dooley privately admitted to himself) scarier reaches of the solar system—towards Jupiter and Ganymede. The Russian ship was already visible through the telescope and he knew, despite the doubts he had expressed to Watt, that they could easily overtake it. True, the *Raskolnikov* had Helmholtz engines five times as powerful as those of the *Doyle*, but it also had twenty times the mass.

Two hours passed during which Oreste became noticeably more puzzled and restless. He too looked through the enhancer, as if to confirm his suspicions, and exclaimed,

"My God, we're practically on top of her!" He turned to Dooley. "You're not really thinking of boarding her?"

"No, I don't think that will be necessary. In fact, it wouldn't even be possible, if he resisted. Despite what you see on television, the boarding equipment can be used only when the other ship is derelict or its crew cooperative. But I want to get close enough to have a tight-beam conversation with our friend Petra without being overheard. There are eavesdroppers everywhere." Oreste looked a little blank at this, so he added, "Also, there's a possibility I want to close out."

He leaned to the radio panel and punched out the call-letters of the *Raskolnikov*, adding the over-ride code Gerasimov had given him.

Almost instantly, guttural sounds broke from the speaker. For a moment both thought they were hearing static, but in the same moment words appeared on the screen of the translator (which had a Russian/English program) beside the speaker:

"Who summons Petra Wetjen?"

Dooley sat back in his chair—so quickly that it seemed to Oreste that he had been "taken aback." He leaned forward again, slowly, his face skeptical:

"I am Thomas Dooley, Chief of Security for the American Sector of the Belt. Do you have an English/Russian program in your computer?"

"I do," was the reply, "but no matter: I speak English."

"After a fashion," muttered Dooley, for the other's words were so thickly encrusted with his native accent that it was hard to discern their original shape. (And on the screen of the translator there appeared: ????????)

The foreign voice went on:

"I speak many languages. I am a student of languages. I speak English very well. I have an excellent grasp of its grammar, but its sounds are awkward to my tongue. Speak to me in English, so that I can savor the sounds. Do not speak to me in any other language."

"I will try not to," promised Dooley. And then: "What do you know of the murder of Carl Neal?"

There was a wait before the reply came. Such a long wait that one might have supposed that the alarmed *Raskolnikov* had leaped forward through a "space warp," as in some old magazine or television story, although it was now plainly visible through the ports. Finally:

"I learn from your question that Carl Neal is dead. This makes me unhappy. Human lives are so short that I grieve to hear that one has been cut shorter still. That is a great wrong. But other deaths have touched me more closely. I grieve for one in particular. If you will forgive me for misquoting the words of your great poet, Gerard Manley Hopkins:

> "'*Tis the blight that man was born for,*
> "'*Tis Petra Wetjen that I mourn for!*'"

Dooley and Oreste exchanged looks of amusement. Dooley leaned even closer to the mike and said, "That's an *English* poet." And then, speaking very distinctly:

"Do you know anything at all relevant to *this* death?"

"I assume that you refer to that of Carl Neal?"

"Assume."

"No, for I did not witness it. Had I been present, it would not have happened. I was inboard this vessel at the time and powerless to act."

"But you were at the scene?"

"I was at the scene."

"You played cards with Carl Neal?"

"Cards? A game of chance? A base submission to contingency? Never!"

"You wrote some words on the surface of a table."

"What were those words?"

"I don't read Russian, but the English translation is 'The Vault of Memory.'"

The *Raskolnikov* again seemed to have leaped ahead many miles. And at last:

"How poor those words sound when broken on the English tongue! How paltry and commonplace! But with what a lilt and cadence they leap from my native tongue, though weighted with feeling...."

"Never mind. Let me bounce another phrase off you: 'The Courts of Justice.'"

"I believe that is prose, and yet I cannot despise it. In addition to my other titles and honors, I am an officer of the law, as I take it you are. If I can assist you in the workings of justice, I shall be glad to do so."

"And I am glad to hear it," said Dooley, with more feeling than he had shown yet. "You *can* assist me. My request is this: That you turn aside from your present course and proceed to Albion, the asteroid on which Carl Neal was killed. I have reason to believe that the person or persons responsible for his death are there, or on the way there, and I may need your help in bringing them to justice. Will you do this?"

"I will," was the reply.

"Quickly, then. For there is no time to be lost. You will have no difficulty?"

"My ship knows the way."

"I will see you there."

Oreste and Dooley turned the *Doyle* manually and then relinquished to the computer the fine-tuning of the flight to the rapidly-scuttling rock that was Albion.

Oreste, after some minutes at the telescope, which was still trained on the *Raskolnikov*, said, "There go the flares! He's doing it. He's slowing and turning the ship."

"If he decided to go on to Ganymede there wouldn't be much

we could do about it. He should be at Albion about twenty minutes after us."

"What do you want to bet he has vodka on his breath?"

"It's a bet."

When they were still half an hour from Albion, Oreste turned the telescope upon the planetoid.

"Good God!" he exclaimed. "It's not possible! Wetjen has gotten there before us!"

"No," said Dooley, who was busying himself at the computer. "That's not the *Raskolnikov*. It's the *S.S. Van Dine*. Senator Bailey is making a courtesy call on the U. N. Observer. A little late, I would say."

Oreste turned back to the instrument, stared through it for several minutes. Dooley heard him breathe the words "Good God!" again, and then, more audibly: "There's the *S.S. Christie!*"

Dooley nodded. "Commissioner Watt has decided to investigate matters at first hand."

"And there's another ship, a small one, at the westward end"—by which he meant, away from the sun—"of the asteroid, but I don't recognize it."

"That would be the *Rendell*," said Dooley. "Madame Neal is paying homage to the place where her beloved husband spent his last hours."

"Three ships," said Oreste, sitting back from the instrument. "Four, if you count Neal's flivver, which is anchored near the igloo. And there will be five and then six when we and the *Raskolnikov* get there." He laughed incredulously. "It's a convention!"

"Yes," muttered Dooley: "'The Gathering of the Suspects.'" Oreste didn't quite pick up on that, but no matter. The Chief Inspector's next remark was more intelligible: "It's about time we suited up."

They moved to the left rear wall of the cabin, which presented them with a blank surface. Dooley touched a button and the metal panel slid downward from sight. Two spacesuits— Westinghouse 1000 models—stood facing them, side by side, from the enclosure.

Both men stared. The curved dark glass of the helmet of the suit to their right reflected them standing there, though somewhat farther apart than they actually were. There was no matching reflection from the suit to their left, because it had no helmet. It had been decapitated.

Dooley said at last, very quietly, "Of course you made the usual equipment check?"

"Of course. I finished an hour before departure. But I had to leave for a few minutes. To see someone about...well, about a personal matter. I may have left the door open."

Dooley's eyes gravitated sideways to Oreste. But it was hardly more than a glance. He turned and made his way back to the computer and positioned himself sideways on the cushioned chair. He sat there for some time without speaking, his face like that of a man at a formal dinner party who has a horrible suspicion that he is going to be sick. Oreste watched him, with growing uneasiness...but when his Chief finally spoke, it was to make some remarks that seemed to him tangential, almost irrelevant.

"Watt and the woman *had* to come in separate vehicles. If they had come in one, cramped together for two or three hours in intimate proximity, it would have aroused the jealousy of Senator Bailey, who I suppose to be her current lover. Do you agree, Lieutenant?"

Oreste nodded his head, without speaking.

"Well!" Dooley slapped his knee. "This is bad, but it's not disastrous. It means only one of us can leave the ship. But, okay, I guess I can handle those three alone. All three are inside the igloo, of course."

Oreste was doubtful. "But if you go in alone, how will I know if you're in trouble? And, even if I do know, even if radio contact is maintained...."

"...even then, you won't be able to come to my rescue? You're right, and if you have any practical suggestion to offer, I'll be glad to hear it. But as far as I can see, we have no choice. I have to go in alone."

"I'm the younger man," hinted Oreste, "and if they offer any physical resistance...."

"Thank you. I'm grateful for your concern. But, you know," he went on, somewhat humorously but with his eyes not moving from Oreste's face, "I have the more imposing authority and am the more likely to overawe them with the indomitable force of my personality."

"But, Chief, they may have that handgun with them!"

"Again, thanks, but that's not an argument for *your* going in. Youth, strength, courage and blond good looks don't count for much against a .45 caliber pistol." Oreste seemed shocked by this, and Dooley added, "But they're not all that likely to have the gun with them. They probably have gotten rid of it."

"But there's this Petra Wetjen fellow who'll be showing up soon. He's an unknown factor."

"You're being awfully insistent, lieutenant! True, there may be some risk; but mine is the greater responsibility, so *I* will be going in. The subject is closed."

Oreste was silent. He watched Dooley with a half smile and a somewhat slack face, as if puzzled by something; then shrugged and dropped his eyes.

CHAPTER NINE

They eased the *S.S. Doyle* to Albion carefully and parked it some yards off, knowing that if they grappled with the rock itself any persons inside the igloo would be forewarned. Radar, the computer and some strategically-placed small jets would keep the ship locked precisely in place. Dooley, coming out of the airlock, black and white in his Westinghouse spacesuit, simply jumped across the intervening gap to the asteroid. He carried an adhesive pad in one hand and clapped it to the rock to keep himself from bouncing away.

It took him less than a minute to gather himself into an upright posture and get his bearings. Edith Neal's elegant flyer, the *Rendell*, was close at hand. Her husband's clodhopper, too humble to have a name, was stationed near the igloo. The familiar *S.S. Christie*, Dooley's usual means of transportation, was furtively peeking into sight above the far end of the asteroid; but, looking beyond and somewhat to the right of the igloo, he could see the huge bulk of the *S.S. Van Dyne* hovering startlingly close—or so it seemed: actually, it was probably twenty miles off.

He started for the igloo, putting each foot down carefully, but the distances were so short that three minutes later he found himself at the tunnel-like projection of the entrance-way. He hesitated...then shrugged and pushed his way through the first of the sphincters. He regretted now that he hadn't brought along his .45—but how likely was it, really, that he would have any need of it?

He entered as quietly as he could, but that wasn't quietly enough. When he stepped through the last of the seals and into the room he found that three faces were already turned towards him. Faces: for all three had removed the helmets of their suits, no doubt the better to promote free and easy conversation. Commissioner Watt had moved one of the inflatable chairs (the fully inflated one) about and was sitting facing the entrance. The helmet of his suit, a NASA SZ80, was balanced on his knee; resting on the table behind him was another helmet, one fitting a Westinghouse 1000 model spacesuit. Sitting on the forward edge of Neal's cot and regarding the intruder with an amused and skeptical expression was a distinguished-looking silver-haired man, probably in his late eighties but in very fine shape. He was wearing a NASA SZ80 also, with the helmet lying on the cot behind him. But placed on the floor at his feet was another helmet: a Westinghouse 1000 model.

And the third? Edith Markley Neal walked towards him from the left and larger side of the igloo. She had removed not only her helmet, but her entire suit, a light-duty GTE, which lay sprawled gracefully and almost seductively on the floor, and was wearing only a red- and silver-striped leotard. She knew where her strengths lay, that woman! Dooley, despite the psychological insulation provided by his spacesuit and despite having seen her before, felt a shock of incredulity and awe. And there came to him from his reading, he thought from the Bible—was it *The Song of Songs?*—a phrase describing a beautiful woman: *"an army with banners flying."*

He turned to look past her, with some unspecific notion of seeing what she had been doing at that end of the igloo, and saw that the curtain that had hid Neal's spacesuit had been pulled aside. The suit still stood where he had last seen it, mounted on the low platform, but now it was topped by a white helmet with a shining black visiplate.

He saw Edith Markley Neal smile. Her lips moved. He couldn't hear her but he imagined she was saying something like, "You see...the purloined helmet. It was in plain sight all along," and he supposed that that would be her defense in court.

But the three were waiting. They must have guessed who he was—certainly she had; although the only identification on his suit, besides the serial number, were the words AMERICAN SECTOR—ASTEROID BELT. He unfastened his helmet and, to show his complete confidence, detached it completely and placed it on the floor by his feet. He could now speak to these people directly, though at the cost of being out of automatic communication with Oreste in the *Doyle*.

His first words were, "The three of you should have compared notes more closely. This superfluity of helmets shows poor teamwork and a slovenly attention to detail." And then, to the man directly in front of him:

"Commissioner Watt, I cannot charge you with being directly involved in the murder of Carl Neal, because I know you were inboard Vesta at the time he was killed. But you have attempted to tamper with the evidence, I suppose to ingratiate yourself with this woman; so I can charge you, and I do charge you, with being an accomplice after the fact. You will consider yourself under arrest."

Watt's complexion darkened dangerously. His upper body shook, his voice vibrated with anger: "Thomas Dooley, you may consider yourself discharged from your position in the Security Forces on grounds of gross insubordination, lying to a superior, negotiating with a representative of a foreign power, trespassing on U. N. property, negligence...."

Dooley ignored him, turned toward the other man. "I presume that you are Senator Bailey."

The older man gave his head a short nod, his expression set in amusement. "Presume."

"Senator Bailey, I charge you with the murder of UN Observer Carl Neal. And, Mrs. Neal, I also charge you with the murder of your husband."

"I'll bet you will!"—it was the voice he had heard that night in Watt's office. "You can't charge me with something that happened when I was seventy-two million miles away at Mars

Station."

"Oh, yes, I can, for you were not at Mars Station when the murder was committed. When you came into Vesta night before last you were in a state of perfect preservation: as fresh as a daisy without a hair out of place; and that wouldn't have been possible if you had just spent five days in the cramped cabin of a tiny flyer. You weren't even five hours in that flyer—more like two. You came directly to Vesta from the Senator's yacht, where you had the attentions of a beautician, a barber, a hairdresser, a medical man, an exercise specialist, and I suppose of every other man on board."

She gave him a look that was the distilled essence of scorn. "Brilliant! And how do you explain away the fact that radar and our radio communications show that my ship was millions of miles away when I first contacted Vesta?"

"The same way any twelve-year-old boy would explain it. As everyone knows, radar identification is very uncertain in the Belt because it's so cluttered. As for the lag in radio communication caused by distance, that can easily be simulated by a computer. I'm not sure it would do me any good to contact Mars Station to check the time of your supposed departure. You may have forestalled me there with some form of bribery...."

Edith Neal smiled.

"...but there is one other thing which could be done, and which I have done. I have taken the liberty of examining the contents of the latrine aboard your flyer." She was watching him now with a horrible fascination. "You're a celestial creature, indeed, Mrs. Neal! You didn't use the toilet once during the five days you supposedly spent on the way from Mars, not even to—how shall I put it?—wee-wee."

She screamed, "Ugh, you filthy beast!" and looked about, as if for something to throw at him. She attempted to seize the helmet lying on the bed behind Senator Bailey, but he, twisting about, snatched it away.

"No violence, my dear!" he warned. "That would be very undignified and unworthy of your beauty. And, besides, it wouldn't do any good. I'm afraid the Chief Inspector has it in his power to make things awkward for us. Very awkward, unless...unless we can persuade him, as a reasonable man, that it's not in the best interests of all concerned, including himself, to pursue this matter further. I presume that you are a reasonable man, Mr. Dooley?"

"Presume."

"I also presume that you are not now in radio communication with some other myrmidon of justice in your flyer, and won't be unless you touch that button at your neckline and speak into the helmet. I hope not, for the fewer ears that hear what I have to say the better. What I am about to propose carries with it an enormous reward. Enormous. But, still," with a smile and a shrug, "we don't want to divide it more ways than we have to, do we?

"Now, Chief Inspector, you may have supposed that Carl Neal's death—you will notice that no vulgar confession is being made here—you may have supposed that his death had something to do with the profits to be made from mining operations in the Asteroid Belt."

"That did occur to me, yes. I know there had to be a large amount of money at stake; otherwise, there wouldn't be any point in a man like that coming out here."

"Quite right. And, true, there are enormous sums to be made from mining the Belt, but there are few profits these days, and sometimes no profits, because the costs are enormous too. Even the Russians, who do everything so much more cheaply than we do, are beginning to feel the pinch. But," watching Dooley carefully, "we in this room are not interested in hacking out large chunks of nickel and iron and then booting them across millions of miles to Earth. We're interested in another kind of material, one that is more easily handled and much more easily transported. Do you have any idea what that might be?"

Dooley thought a moment. "Information."

"Precisely. Information. Not about the Belt, which has pretty well been scoured clean of any interest it possesses, but about what lies beyond the Belt."

"Ganymede."

"Right, again!" said the Senator, with undisguised admiration. "There's a Russian named Petra Wetjen who made a documentary on Ganymede that was funded by the National Geographic Society and the Russian Government. The Simple Ganymedans at Work and Play—that sort of thing. But, while taping it, he came across something unexpected. He discovered that the Ganymedans have a system of writing—everyone had thought they had only an oral culture—and that their written history goes back a long way."

Watt, who had been fidgeting, could contain himself no longer.

"A long way! That's the understatement of the century. We know it goes back at least three million years."

"At least," agreed the Senator. "Our written history goes back only five thousand years, so we're pikers, johnny-come-latelies, compared to the Ganymedans. Wetjen learned that they have a great poem of many thousands of lines, something like *The Iliad*, I suppose, describing their Golden Age. He called it *The Golgonoosiad*, but they have another name, roughly translated as *The Vault of History....*"

"*Memory...,*" suggested Dooley.

"*...Memory*: right. It seems that they regard this epic poem of theirs as a kind of sacred work, not to be cheaply bandied about; but they came to know and like Petra Wetjen and saw no harm in telling him of it. And he saw no harm in mentioning it to Mr, Neal, whom he had known in Moscow some years ago."

"Yes," said Dooley, "and Mr. Neal saw no harm in mentioning it to Mrs. Neal."

"Quite right." The Senator smiled sadly. "And she saw fit to let some of her very closest and oldest friends in on the news,"

"And all of them lovers of classic literature."

"No crappy jokes, Dooley," said Watt. "Do you have any idea what we've got here?" He leaned forward and said with profound conviction: "*We've got a Best Seller here!*"

"Probably more than one," said the Senator.

"And a television mini-series," said Edith Neal.

"And a movie or two," said Watt. "This thing is *big*!"

"Do you have any idea what a Best Seller makes these days?" asked Edith Neal, with a fine edge of scorn for any possible ignorance he might show on the subject.

Dooley had no idea; but the Senator came to his rescue.

"Any book that gets to be Number 1 on *The New York Times Best Seller List* must sell at least thirty million copies, and many books have done so. Of course today, with the world-wide spread of English as a *lingua franca*, a Best Seller is a global phenomenon; one or two books, such as Newbegin's *Dirty Bathrobe*, have been known to sell thirty million in China alone."

Watt said in an awe-struck tone, "We estimate that there may be as much as half a billion dollars to be made out of a book on this subject. A *book*—without even mentioning the movie, television and video rights."

"And it's not just a short-term deal," went on the Senator, persuasively. "Our idea is to secure the material and copyright it in our names on Earth. There would be absolutely no use of it by anyone for three or four generations to come without a fee being paid to us. Do you have children, Chief Inspector? No? Well, it's not too late, especially if you return to Earth as a rich man. If you join us in this venture, I promise you that not only your children but their children's children will be very rich indeed."

Watt made a sound that was like the primeval ancestor of laughter. "And if you don't come in with us, what will you have? That paltry and contemptible pension which even now you are looking forward to as the reward of a lifetime of work and risk for the public."

"One fourth for you," said the Senator, looking around at the others for agreement.

"One fourth," said Watt, in a take-it-or-leave-it tone.

"One fourth," said Edith Markley Neal, sweetening the figure with a smile that seemed to hint at all sorts of additional benefits.

Dooley looked down at the floor. "Tempting," he said at last.

"Very tempting. But, you know"—raising his eyes to theirs, eyes that they saw were tired and disgusted; "murder rather sticks in my craw. Why did you have to kill Carl Neal? Wouldn't he go along with the deal?"

"He was a weakling and a fool!" said Neal's wife, her voice seething with contempt. "He didn't have the stomach for a little necessary violence."

The Senator raised an alarmed hand towards her. "My dear, you have just handed this man a dagger—a dagger pointed at your heart."

Dooley looked down at the floor again. He said, "Allow me to toy with the dagger a bit." They waited. And he went on,

"I'm puzzled. I know you killed Carl Neal...but I also seem to sense that you killed Petra Wetjen. All the signs point in that direction. And yet, it cannot be. It simply cannot be!" Looking up, he saw that he had their undivided attention: all three were so fascinated by what he was saying that they seemed to have stopped breathing. "Shall I tell you," he asked, "what my theory would be, if it weren't for one small detail?

"It is this: that for some reason you found it necessary to eliminate Wetjen. Perhaps it was because he demanded a larger share of the loot than you were willing to give him. Or perhaps it was because he was an honorable and upright man—forgive my language!— who refused to go along with your plan to exploit the sacred traditions of the Pugs for your private gain. But, for whatever reason, you killed him. You then placed his body aboard his fully-automated ship, the *Raskolnikov*, programmed its controls in such a way that it would fulfill its already prearranged functions, such as stopping by Vesta for supplies—that would give you a wonderful alibi, wouldn't it? for everyone would assume that he was alive and well on his ship several days after his murder—and then have the ship move on and disappear forever: into the proverbial Red Spot of Jupiter, say, or into the outer reaches."

Watt broke in with a scoff. "Waste a two billion dollar ship! Who could bring themselves to do that?"

"*You* could, Commissioner, if it would save you a few years in an Earthside prison. And, besides, what difference can it make to you how valuable the ship was? There's no way in which you could gain possession of it."

"But why," murmured the Senator, as if reproving an absurdity, "would we kill Wetjen? Wouldn't that be like killing the goose that laid the golden egg? It's the Ganymedans who have what we want...and our only connection with them is through him."

"Yes," admitted Dooley, "that's a puzzler. But I think I can come up with an answer to that one, too. Your ship, Senator, the *S.S. Van Dyne*, is an exact duplicate of Wetjen's ship, the *Raskolnikov*. All you would have to do is to visit Ganymede, tell the Pugs that Wetjen had been prevented from coming, or was sick aboard the ship, and request the materials they had promised to give him. And, also, they had of course met the technicians who were with Wetjen when he was making the famous documentary and you could trot out a few of those. Perhaps they're aboard your ship at this very moment, Senator? I rather think they are. No: Petra Wetjen would have been very useful to you as an ally and intermediary, but if he seriously balked you could dispense with him without giving up your plans. And how could you dispense with him except by murdering him?

"That, anyway," he concluded, "would have been my theory."

"Would have been?" said Bailey. "But you have abandoned it? Because of a small detail?"

"Yes."

"And what," asked the Senator, smiling, "was that small detail?"

"It's that Petra Wetjen is still very much alive. I *know*, because I had a little talk with him an hour or so ago."

He saw their faces freeze again, their eyes widen and stare. So chilling was the effect of his words that he half-expected to see the warm breath issuing from their mouths and nostrils become visible in the air of the cabin.

But he showed them no mercy. He pressed on:

"I persuaded him to come here and he's on his way. He'll be here at any moment. In fact, if I'm not mistaken, that's him now."

For the floor had moved. It now swayed sideways and then dropped.

There was an exclamation, curse and scream from Bailey, Watt and Edith Neal. There was a queasy see-sawing motion, a scurrying of small objects, a metallic scrape and clatter as the helmet on the table slid and crashed to the floor...which righted itself and pressed upward under their feet, as if they were in a rising elevator. In the next moment, the sensation of movement and weight vanished, and Dooley knew that the artificial-gravity field of .the *Raskolnikov* had been switched off. The pilot must have brought the great ship into almost direct contact with the asteroid.

A whimpering Edith Neal picked herself up from the floor. Both Senator Bailey and Commissioner Watt were on their feet. Edith, her eyes wide and dark in her pale face, came forward, as if fascinated, towards the entrance. Watt and Bailey made one or two shuffling steps in that direction also...like sleep-walkers, or thought Dooley, like the characters in some old film about the "Living Dead"...or (could it be?) like those who expect to see the Living Dead?

CHAPTER TEN

Not two minutes passed before they felt an indefinable vibration through the floor and knew that someone was fumbling with the outer seal of the entrance. This was followed by rustling sounds as of someone pushing his way through the successive shutters. Dooley was eager to see "this giant among men," as Gerasimov had called him, but he kept one eye on his fellow inmates too: saw them watching as raptly as Eskimos might at the expected entrance of a polar bear into their igloo. And what shouldered its way through the last seal was not, at first glance, unlike a polar bear; for it was large and white and walking on all fours.

The newcomer stood up and Dooley saw why he had had to crawl when he came through the tunnel—for the occupant of the spacesuit had to be about eight feet tall and he would surely have weighed five hundred pounds on Earth, if not more.

He noticed that the suit itself was a Gorky. There was a red star on the right breast and various Cyrillic letters on the left, but no other identification. It had, of course, been custom-made for its outsized wearer, and it was made even more grotesque, by American standards, by a disproportionately large and cumbersome backpack.

Edith, Watt, and Bailey seemed to be in a state of shock... powerless to move as the space-suited figure lumbered forward like some upright Russian bear. It stopped at the table. One hand came up, fumbled at the catches and latches of the helmet, lifted it just a crack. Dooley thought to hear sounds like a bear sniffing the air, but, after a moment's hesitation, the helmet was thrown all the way back.

The head revealed to view was covered by an old-fashioned Russian cosmonaut's brown leather helmet. The face itself was broad and white as snow. Some citizens of the sun-starved Belt perversely boasted of their pallor, but all other pallors paled before this. The eyes were large and filmed over, the pupils very large, as if dilated by drugs, and very black. The nostrils were prominent and—Dooley could hardly believe this detail—plugged like an unborn child's. It was definitely not a handsome face and it wasn't made any handsomer by apparently having suffered some mutilating accident: for an ugly scar, raised, prominent and raw, like burn-tissue, ran up the left side of his neck and face to the corner of his mouth—it looked to Dooley like a millipede trying to crawl into the mouth.

The silence was broken by an hysterical laugh from Edith Neal. "You're the ugliest son-of-a-bitch I've ever seen in my life."

The Visitor turned his head and looked her up and down.

"I do not understand," he said, forming the words carefully but with his pronunciation thickened by an unfamiliar accent; "I do not understand that phrase you have used"—he must have meant "son-of-a-bitch"—"but I know the meaning of the super-lative 'ugliest' and know that you mean to insult me. I take no offense. I can feel only pity for someone as deformed as you are."

It was Edith Neal's turn to stare, her mouth slightly open.

Dooley's face cleared, as if some small problem had been solved. But what he said was, "It would seem that ugliness is in the eye of the beholder."

The giant turned his eye towards him, as if to test that notion. But what *he* said was, "You are Thomas Dooley?"

"I am Chief Inspector Dooley. Tell me, where is Petra Wetjen?"

"Alas! You will find no one who answers to that name, though you search through all Golgonooza and Ramashanshan. But, if by "Petrawetjen" you mean that clumsy contraption, now *kaput*, which so pathetically mocks him, you will find it aboard the vessel that was once the pride of Petrawetjen."

Watt cried out, as if stung beyond endurance, "What in Hell does 'this Russian bastard' mean?"

"He means," said Dooley, not taking his eyes from 'this Russian bastard,' "that Petra Wetjen is dead and his corpse is inboard the *Raskolnikov*. And who, sir," he asked, "are *you*?"

"I," said the newcomer, drawing himself up to his full height, "am the Keeper of the Vault."

There was a long silence as all digested the implications of this announcement...a silence at last broken by an awe-struck murmur from Senator Bailey:

"*The Vault of Memory.*"

The Ganymedan bowed in his direction.

And then Edith Neal, with another laugh, one that went up the musical scale in distinct notes, said, "You mean...you're a *librarian*!"

Dooley instantly resented the implied slight, on Heloise's behalf. For, after all, what was Heloise—what would she have been in a 1940s movie?—except a librarian? But the Pug was either gratified or magnanimous. He bowed again:

"I indeed have the honor of being a member of that noble profession."

The Senator said, "*The Vault of Memory* is the great epic of... Golgonooza?"

"Yes. My beloved Petrawetjen called it The *Golgonoosiad.*"

"And Golgonooza is the place we call Ganymede?"

The Keeper of the Vault's snort of contempt threatened to blow the plugs from his nostrils. "No, indeed! That is Ramashanshan, a poor place, our temporary dwelling, whose history is fittingly told only in prose. *The Golgonoosiad* is in verse and tells the story of our Mother Planet, the true home of our race. You wrong us when you call us Ganymedans, for Ganymede did not give us birth. Ah, how happy we were on Golgonooza! We stood then in the light of the sun and were warmed by balmy breezes. Now we live our days in endless shadow and uncongenial coolness."

Dooley asked, "And just where is Golgonooza?"

The Ganymedan gave a loud, hoarse cry, like that of a large animal in pain, and spread wide his arms. *"It is HERE!"*

Dooley, Watt, Edith Neal and the Senator looked about at the interior of the mean hut in which Carl Neal had eked out his last days and then, baffled, at each other and at their visitor.

"This," said the Ganymedan, "is what remains of our sacred planet. This, and such other fragments as Vesta, Eohippus, Hermes, Ceres. What you call the Asteroid Belt is the debris of Golgonooza."

There was another silence, which was broken again by the Senator's quiet voice. "There used to be a theory that the asteroid belt was composed of the fragments of what was once a planet, a fifth Earth-scale planet, in an orbit between Mars and Jupiter, and that it was destroyed by a collision with another body. But that theory was discarded more than a century ago."

"Prematurely, it would seem," said Dooley.

Bailey shook his white head in wondering dismay. "Imagine: The destruction of an entire world. What a terrible accident!"

But their visitor wouldn't allow that. He cried out again, not as loud as before, but this time his voice was hoarse with rage. "It was no accident! It was *murder!*"—a cry that awakened a curious echo inside the hut. "We did not know that jealous eyes were watching us from afar, malicious eyes that envied us our happiness. They were the eyes of the Old Ones, Dwellers in the Far Night, who had visited us long before and had been sent away as spiteful creatures. They hurled against us a great rock that struck Golgonooza and shattered it to bits. All this is told in *The Everlasting Wrong*, the Fifth Book of *The Golqonoosiad*. A few of us escaped in a ship that had been left behind by the Old Ones and fell upon Ramashanshan. This is told in the Sixth Book, *The Exodus*. On Ramashanshan we took such shelter as we could find and have bided our time ever since." He added, "I can, if you wish," favoring them all with a hopeful, filmy gaze, "recite the first three thousand lines of *The Everlasting Wrong.*"

"Some other time," suggested Dooley. "At the moment we have more pressing business. What is your connection with"— he waved a hand—"these people here?"

"A sorry one. The noble Petrawetjen had meant to give *The Golgonoosiad* to the people of your world as a gift...or practically a gift, for we would receive in exchange only Homer, the Bible, Dante, Shakespeare, and Dickens. He came to this Relict, which you call Albion, to discuss the matter with his friend Carl Neal, and with his friend's friends. I waited in his ship, in a special apartment filled with breathable air. He was not to mention my presence until his talk with his friend and his friend's friends was concluded. Then, and only then, was I to be introduced. He said it would be a *coup de théâtre*—a phrase from another of the languages he spoke and I speak. I waited. I may or may not have waited a long time. I am not afflicted with that disease you call impatience. And then there came into the *Raskolnikov* and into my range of vision—for, though sequestered, I had means to see—three persons who carried with them something that filled me with such grief and rage it robbed me of my senses. It was the detritus of Petrawetjen. Oh! The loss I felt when I knew that I would never again hear the voice of my friend and teacher Petrawetjen. There was no flaw in that man! He was beyond compare. Where he was, there was a balmy breeze from Golgonooza."

"Who were the three persons?"

"I saw the faces of two only. One was this man with the white hair. Another was this individual with the long red hair, whom I now suppose to be one of your fertile females. I recognize them because they removed their helmets when they came into the ship. There was with them a man who did not remove his helmet. He moved about and waved his arms violently, as if he were angry. He may or may not be the same angry man as this angry man"—indicating Watt.

Watt opened his mouth and something like a squall came out—a roaring wind with minute drops. "You lie! I was nowhere near here when the murders occurred."

"You fool!" said Senator Bailey, with profound weariness.

Dooley said, "No, I don't think it was this man. The helmet of the man you saw was removed a little later...when he was *outside* the ship."

He turned and looked over the Senator and Edith Neal. Looked them over slowly, ignoring the apoplectic Watt as beneath notice. "We know why Petra Wetjen was killed. He refused to go along with your scheme to seize control of *The Golgonoosiad* for yourselves alone. And," he went on, addressing Edith Neal directly, "I know why your husband was killed. He didn't mind making a few million dollars—after all, what harm could his sharing the rights to this ancient epic poem do anyone? But he hadn't counted on murder and he drew the line at murder. After you and the Senator killed Wetjen, your husband made a nuisance of himself. The two of you saw that if he went on in that way, you could wind up in prison.

"And I know *how* he was killed. The helmet of the Westinghouse spacesuit can be removed only if its wearer tightens his left hand into a fist and undoes the fastenings with his right hand. My guess is that you, Senator, struck him while the three of you were standing outside on the surface of Albion and he instinctively responded in the manner of any American male: he made a fist. And while he was in that defensive posture, his loving wife clung to him—and undid his helmet.

"Your husband died a horrible death, Mrs. Neal, before your very eyes. But maybe it's a little easier to watch the second time. You'd already seen Petra Wetjen's lungs, heart and eyes rupture when you removed *his* helmet...which was easier to remove, it being a Gorky.

"Why," sneered Watt, "it's almost as if you were there!"

But Dooley ignored him. He pressed on, speaking with clairvoyant conviction.

"After you murdered Carl Neal, you carried his body back inside this place and arranged that little tableau to make it look as if he'd been killed by a stray meteor punching a double hole through the igloo. You were delighted by your ingenuity and giggled to each other about it—oh, yes, you did!—and then you received a shock, the most terrible shock of your lives. You discovered that what you had with you was the wrong helmet. I would give a great deal to have seen your faces at that moment— the moment you at last noticed those Cyrillic letters. For you had brought with you the helmet to Wetjen's suit, not Neal's. They had been stripped of their helmets on the same patch of ground, outside the airlock of Wetjen's ship, and you had tossed the wrong helmet into the ship before the lock closed and it went on its predestined and automated way to Vesta and points beyond. You didn't know that there was a passenger aboard, this gentleman here, Wetjen's *protégé*, whom he had taught to navigate the ship and who had witnessed the immediate aftermath of the murders.

"What to do? That was your problem. Here you'd been left holding a Russian-made helmet that couldn't possibly fit the Westinghouse spacesuit. And having the wrong helmet wasn't just as bad as having no helmet. It was worse: for the presence of the wrong helmet suggested premeditation. More than that: it pointed to the possibility of a second murder—for where had *that* helmet come from?—and even perhaps to the person murdered, once Wetjen's involvement became known.

"My guess is that you had quite a discussion about all this, with many recriminations, but it ended by your doing the only thing you could do. You carried the Gorky helmet away. It is now either hidden on the Senator's yacht, or, more likely, it was flung into space, to be lost among the minutia of the Belt. Perhaps it's in orbit around Albion now."

Watt sneered again. "What a load! What a tissue of speculations! You haven't a shred of evidence to support any of that."

But Dooley took no heed. The only responses that mattered where those of Edith Neal and Senator Bailey. Both were watching him with an unnatural, almost preternatural, steadiness, without the slightest flicker of expression. He knew he was right. And probably right in every particular.

CHAPTER ELEVEN

He turned back to the Ganymedan. "Your testimony as to what you saw inside the *Raskolnikov*, together with what evidence I have and to what these three have confessed, is enough to indict Senator Bailey and Mrs. Neal and it may be enough to convict them. Will you agree to testify before the Circuit Court on Vesta?"

There was a gentle laugh from the Senator. "That's nonsense!" He made an easy movement where he sat, indicating a return of amused self-confidence. "Your so-called evidence and our so-called confessions will never stand up under cross-examination. I think you know that...."

He was right. Dooley did.

"...and, as for what he saw, let me tell you that I have had forty years of experience as an advocate and a judge and I *know* that no jury composed of human beings will ever send Edith Neal or me to prison on the word of this grotesque creature."

And Dooley knew that too. But he said, "My job is not to convict you. That's the business of the Court. My job is simply to bring you to trial."

The Senator smiled. "That must be a deeply satisfying work-ethos, Chief Inspector."

Dooley naturally resented the contempt; and yet he felt something like respect for this man, wearily corrupt though he was. But he had not yet received his reply from the Keeper of the Vault, and when that came it changed everything.

"I will not testify in your court, for your court has no authority here. This is Golgonooza. We, the children of Golgonooza, have endured much. We have watched you chipping and pocking away at our sacred planet, dribbling it sunward. We have said nothing but have looked on indulgently as you enriched yourselves with the crumbs that fell from what should have been our table. We have bided our time and will yet a while longer. But in this matter of Petrawetjen, the Beloved of Ramashanshan, we must speak: not only for him who can no longer speak, but because the ghostly soil of Golgonooza has been polluted by his murder. The three men responsible"—indicating Watt, Bailey, and Edith Neal with his massive thumb—"must come to see that they have committed a great wrong, and they cannot see that until they have been purged of the poisons of greed, selfishness, and impatience. They must be brought to the Chamber of Remorse on Ramashanshan."

Watt cried out again, "What does the bastard mean?"

"He means," said Dooley, "that the crime was committed in his jurisdiction and that you must be taken to Ganymede for rehabilitation."

There were cries of outrage from Watt and Edith Neal. The Senator said nothing. Dooley turned towards him and, speaking very quietly, for his ears only, said,

"Senator Bailey, prepare yourself for the worst. If this guy decides to hustle the three of you out of here by the scruffs of your necks, I don't see how I can stop him. He outweighs me."

Bailey said, even more quietly, "He's a Majority of One, but I think I'll cast a dissenting vote, anyway. In fact, a veto."

He reached back and removed something from under the helmet on the bed behind him: a .45 caliber pistol. No doubt, it was the same pistol he had used to punch a hole through the igloo.

He raised the gun. There was an explosive sound, very loud, but—given the acoustics of the place—without resonance. A dark hole appeared in the lower right breast of the Gorky spacesuit.

The Ganymedan reached out, took hold of the pistol, and

gently removed it from the Senator's grasp. He placed two large fingers on the top of the gun, a third at the back of the stock, and with his remaining finger—an opposing thumb—bent the barrel backwards to a ninety-degree angle; and then, with a courteous gesture, handed the gun back to the man who had shot him. Bailey contemplated the gun in his hand, then raised his eyes to the dark spot on the white spacesuit. All four humans stared at the spot, three of them hopefully. It was an ugly splotch, as if someone had stubbed out an old-fashioned cigar there...but nothing like blood appeared.

The Ganymedan said, addressing himself to Dooley, as if to a fellow officer of the law:

"'Have no fear. The projectile missed both my hearts and harmed no vital organ. It was to me little more than the sting of one of your flying insects would be to you—painful and annoying, but not decisive."

And then to the others: "Prepare yourselves now for the voyage to Ramashanshan."

"They're not going," said Dooley. "These persons are my prisoners and, as such, under my protection. Also, they are American citizens on what is now recognized as American soil and cannot be taken away by you or by the representative of any foreign power."

"A pity. I will be sorry to use force, for I must later cleanse my soul of the offense."

Dooley was baffled and dismayed. He saw no way in which he could deal with the huge bulk and awesome strength of the Ganymedan. The Senator sat silent. Watt turned upon Dooley a look of abject appeal. Seeing no hope there, he sank wordlessly down upon the chair he had recently occupied: the fully-inflated one. He actually seemed to be pale. He asked, very faintly, "How long would we be there?"

The Ganymedan replied, "I do not understand that question. On Ramashanshan we do not parsimoniously parcel out the years."

A loud wail of anguish was torn from Edith Neal,

"Darling! Darling! Do something!"

Dooley looked instantly, automatically, at Bailey and Watt and was shocked to see that this agonizing cry had brought neither of her lovers to his feet. Heartless bastards! For he himself—although he certainly wasn't her darling—was horribly stricken by that desperate cry for help.

He saw Edith turn and totter away from the Ganymedan, towards the farther end of the igloo, saw her agonized gestures ludicrously reflected in the dark visiplate of the Westinghouse spacesuit, and he heard once again that heartrending cry,

"Darling, help me!"

He actually took a step or two after her, hardly knowing what he meant to do, hardly knowing what he could do; knowing only that nothing human could be immune to such an appeal.

The Westinghouse 1000 Model Spacesuit was not immune. It stepped down off the small platform on which it was mounted and stalked towards them.

Dooley felt an immense and curious shock—curious in that there squirmed under it some nondescript dismay.

The suit stopped directly in front of Edith Neal and a few yards from him. It raised its left glove and clenched it into a menacing fist...while the right glove fumbled at the fastenings at the neckline.

The helmet was thrown back and Dooley looked upon a familiar face.

He literally staggered as the floor once again seemed to drop away from beneath his feet. It was as if the igloo, the whole asteroid, had tilted.

"Ralph!" he gasped.

"You fool!" said Edith Neal. "You shouldn't have removed your helmet. You'd be more useful to me if he didn't know who you were."

Phelps said, "I had to remove it, sweetheart. Otherwise," and he dipped a hand into the neckline of the suit, "otherwise, I couldn't have gotten hold of this." And he fished out a .45 caliber pistol, which his friend thought to recognize as the one he had left behind in a drawer in his room.

Dooley felt rage, disgust, a sickening pity.

"Ralph," he said gently, extending his hand, "give me back the gun. If you do, this will be forgotten. You just lost your head, that's all. You've been...." He groped for a word, came up with one that hadn't been used in decades: "...seduced. I'll see to it that you're not prosecuted. There are ways...."

"That's not good enough," said Phelps, and Dooley saw that he was still in the elated state he had seen on Rockland Boulevard. "I can't permit my Edith to be taken away to that dismal, frozen place."

"Can you mean Ramashanshan?" asked the Ganymedan, with what sounded like a touch of patriotic indignation: perhaps like some other persons who disparage their own countries, he didn't want anyone else to do so. "Nevertheless, she *will* be taken there. I have no fear of that weapon. All my organs are redundant, and even if they weren't, I would not be deterred."

"Oh, its not *you* I mean to shoot," said Phelps, his moon-like face glowing with good-humored confidence. "I'm going to shoot Senator Bailey and Commissioner Watt."

The Senator and Watt rose to their feet, stood staring at Phelps in astounded disbelief. The Ganymedan did quite the opposite. He collapsed. He sank downward slowly, his large arms hanging at his sides. Sank down and squatted on the floor, sitting partly on his heels and partly on the outsized backpack of his suit. Dooley was reminded of the moment when the chair, now in front of him, had deflated...and when he himself had deflated.

The Ganymedan said, "You have defeated me. I can do nothing that will result in the loss of a life."

"My darling Edith and I," said Phelps, "are going to take the Senator's yacht back to Earth. I'll take the Senator along: he may come in handy."

"Take me too," pleaded Watt.

"Oh, I think not," said Phelps, with a sly sideways glance at the man. "Edith tells me that her memories of her friendship with you are now very painful to her and I'm sure she wouldn't want them revived."

Edith laughed with delight. "How true! How true!"

Dooley said, "I can't let you do this, Ralph. You're not leaving here except in my custody."

The old Phelps would have been daunted by that; but this new Phelps, so much like the old in mere physical appearance, was not in the least ruffled. He smiled, turned to the Ganymedan and said,

"If this man tries to stop me, you are to seize and hold him."

The Keeper nodded. "I will do as you say. You are master here."

"Yes, I am master here," repeated Phelps, relishing the unaccustomed phrase.

"You're a genius!" cried Edith, doing a rapid little two-step and clapping her hands like a child. "You're a hero! You are my Sir Lancelot, my Galahad! You have saved me from a fate worse than death, and oh! oh! oh! what rewards you shall have!"

"One moment," said Dooley, raising a finger. "There's a little thing I must attend to"—in the familiar tone of someone excusing himself at a social gathering.

But, as they stared, he stepped not into the loo of the igloo but into the adjacent kitchenette, where he was hidden from their view by a partition. He tore a yard of papercloth from the dispenser and turned on the faucet of the sink: water gushed towards its recycling throat. He wet the towel thoroughly and draped it over his face and head. The thin, wet folds clung to his forehead, nose and chin—he could barely breathe, but he could see well enough through its porous tissues.

And when he stepped out into the larger room again, he carried concealed in his right hand the dormant sharp edge of a Jiffy vibro-canopener that he had plucked from the magnetic grip of its holder.

The others gaped as he moved towards them with the wet towel molded to his features.

The Senator groaned, "Oh, my God! He's gone mad!"

Edith Markley Neal danced away in alarm. "Kill him! Kill him!" she sang.

But of course Phelps hesitated...and Dooley fell upon the partly-inflated chair beside the table and slit it open from top to bottom in one disemboweling gash with the can-opener. Lying on the chair and squeezing it in his arms like an accordion, he forced its gaseous contents out into the room.

Acrid odors, nauseous and stinging, polluted the air: for this was the chair that Petra Wetjen had brought with him from Ganymede and had sat in while playing cards with Carl Neal.

There was a moment's incomprehension and then pandemonium. An hysterical scream from Edith Neal. Shouts, curses, gasps and moans from the men. A frantic hubbub of scrambling feet transmitted to Dooley through the fiber-board floor.

Rising from the flattened chair and looking through the wet towel, Dooley saw that his friend Ralph had dropped the gun and had reeled away, covering his face with his gloved hands. He saw Watt huddling on the floor, hunched into a ball. He saw Bailey desperately trying to re-attach the helmet of his space-suit—but he had picked up the Westinghouse and not the NASA SZ80. And he saw that Edith had tried to get out of the igloo through the entrance-tunnel. She had fallen and was lying half-inside the first chamber, with her shapely rump and legs still in view—fortunately: because if she had succeeded in making it to the outside without a suit or helmet she would have found it even more difficult to breathe...and, thought Dooley, she would have learned what it was like to die as her husband had died.

Only the Ganymedan had risen to the occasion. That is, he had risen to his feet and had spread his arms wide as in a transport of joy. His mouth was open, as if he were breathing in delicious odors, and Dooley now saw that the ugly scar crawling up the side of his face terminated inside his mouth as a truncated white tube. He saw too that the Ganymedan's eyes were no longer bleared and glazed. They were clear and open—for, like a camel, he had a double set of eyelids, transparent lids beneath the regular lids, and these too were now retracted.

The Keeper of the Vault was breathing the air of Ramashanshan and of Golgonooza.

But not for long. The air-conditioning unit of the igloo was making urgent noises and was already cleaning the alien gases from the atmosphere.

There followed several minutes more of sobs, moans, curses, sniffles and coughs from the other humans...and a few more before they quite realized that they had perhaps over-reacted. Watt got to his feet. Edith picked herself up and stood entirely inside the room. She was teary-eyed...but so were her three lovers.

The Ganymedan remained standing. But his mouth was closed now and his eyes were once again sicklied o'er with the pale cast of memory.

Dooley leisurely, almost negligently, stripped the wet paper cloth from his face and stooped to pick up his gun.

CHAPTER TWELVE

He waved the gun casually. "The cards are now in my hand," he said to the Ganymedan, who perhaps didn't fully understand the expression. "If you attempt to remove these people, I will shoot this man"—indicating Senator Bailey—"who is responsible for the deaths of at least two persons."

Did the Ganymedan smile? Or was it just a quirk of his very thin lips? Perhaps the tube inserted there hurt his mouth?

"I do not believe you, Chief Inspector Dooley. You would never kill this man, except to save an innocent life from otherwise certain extinction."

Dooley saw what he had to do. He turned and pointed the gun directly at Senator Bailey's chest...and the Senator smiled.

He said, "You would have to kill me. Medical science being what it is these days, merely putting a bullet through my lung wouldn't have a very persuasive effect. You would have to kill me outright to show you mean business and then threaten to kill more before this creature would let the others go. Perhaps you should. If you don't, what sort of life will I have for...who knows how many years. Death might be preferable. Kill me and save the day for these others. If you can."

And Dooley, staring at the Senator's handsome face, knew that he couldn't. He felt a pang of mortification and self-contempt. He knew that Ralph could do it. *Even* Ralph could do it. But, then, Ralph was in love. He would snuff out the Senator's life for the sake of his beloved Edith...and then give no thought, as Dooley had to, to future Boards of Inquiry.

He sighed and stuck the pistol into the instrument pouch at his right side.

The Ganymedan looked about. "It is time. All must come with me, except the Chief of the Inspectors."

A light dimmed in the faces of them all as they recognized and accepted the hopelessness of their situation. It was over. Bailey and Watt began putting on the helmets to their suits, their eyes vacant, their fingers moving mechanically.

Phelps came forward to Edith Neal's side. "My sweetheart, I cannot rescue you. But at least we will be together in the months and years to come on Jupiter's icy moon."

She said, "You old fool!" with a look that would have shriveled a bouquet of flowers. "Why do you think I would want to spend any part of my life, even an hour, with an old goat like you?"

Phelps' asteroid pallor deepened. He struggled to speak, but at first could find no words. And then, lamely:

"Old? Why, by modern standards...."

She told him in no uncertain words just what it was he could do with "modern standards," and then moved to the middle of the room to put on her GTE spacesuit.

Before she stepped and wiggled her way into it, Dooley saw her turn a slow wistful and curiously speculative gaze around the interior of the igloo. Did it occur to her at that moment that she could have made this mean hutch into a corner of paradise for some lucky man—her husband, say—had her soul been bent in that direction? Perhaps it did.

Dooley turned away from her and was startled to encounter, very close, the despairing, accusatory face of Ralph Phelps.

"I'll never write that book on you now, Tom. And why should I? You're not worthy. A detective hero should be the pure embodiment of the spirit of ratiocination, but you—*you* never rise completely above personal concerns. Can you imagine Sherlock Holmes looking forward to his Christmas vacation or worrying about his pension?"

Dooley said, "I'm a little disappointed in me too, Ralph." He put his hand on Phelps' shoulder and said to the Ganymedan, "Perhaps you can spare me this fellow? He has led a blameless life until now, when he was subject to a temptation few males of our species could resist. Perhaps you can make some allowance for the biological drives of another race?"

The Keeper of the Vault eyed Dooley. He said, "You have a strange notion of virtue." He fingered his chin in a human-like gesture of speculative indecision. "Perhaps you too should come with us for moral purification...?"

Dooley's hand rested on the pouch at his side. "I think not. I have other plans for the next few decades."

The Ganymedan glanced at the pouch. His mouth twitched again.

"As you wish," he said, and raised and lowered the helmet of his own suit into place. The bullet of a .45 might be to him no more than the sting of a wasp...but perhaps, like most people, he didn't really care all that much for wasp-stings.

All were ready. The six filed out of the igloo through the entrance-tunnel. The giant Ganymedan led the way, walking on all fours and looking very much like a white elephant with too much castle on its back. The defeated Dooley brought up the ignominious rear. Like a thrifty housekeeper, he threw the switches that turned off the lights and other systems as he left.

Outside, on the giddy surface of the planetoid, all looked about, all uneasily conscious of how lightly they were held to the ground, all trembling inwardly with awe in the personal presence of the stars.

Dooley, as he came out into the open, saw that he had been right in supposing that the Ganymedan had brought his ship into almost direct contact with the asteroid. He had parked it on the very doorstep of Albion; in other words, on the horizon, a hundred yards away. The pilot who had accomplished that feat turned and indicated to his captives the lighted airlock, which he had left open, although they could hardly have escaped seeing it: for it was glowing like a harvest moon and littering the choppy ground before it with husks of light.

Dooley looked to his left and saw that the sister ship was now much closer, but inert. When he looked to his right, expecting to see the *S.S. Doyle*, he experienced an unpleasant start of surprise, for the ship was not where he had left it.

Of course the radio link had been re-established the moment he had sealed his helmet, and he now said, with just a touch of alarm, "Oreste?" No reply. "Oreste, where are you?" Silence. "Why the devil don't you answer!"

But his attention was called back to what was happening directly in front of him. Four diminutive-looking figures were being shepherded by what seemed a life-sized figure into the airlock of the giant ship. The Westinghouse 1000 model space-suit stumbled on the threshold, picked itself up and looked back at him. A horrible feeling, wordless and paralyzing, sank a shaft into Dooley's soul. He supposed that the four would be preserved alive and not mistreated...but would they still be recognizably human when next seen? Maybe not. The lock rolled shut, hiding them from view, and Dooley stood in darkness, except for the light of the stars. Behind him, the translucent fabric of the igloo was dark.

He was jolted by a sudden fear. He turned and stumbled back to the entrance-tunnel of the igloo. Taking hold of the rim, he wedged himself partly inside the sphincter of the first chamber; for if the Ganymedan turned on his artificial gravity before, or just after, moving the ship away, he would be yanked off the island. And, with Oreste gone, what would happen then? Could he count on the crew of the corrupt Senator's yacht to rescue him?

The large ship slid silently away, but it was some distance off before he felt the tug. It slapped him against the inside rim of the tunnel; but what almost caused him to lose his grip was not the gross physical attraction of the ship but something he saw. As the huge mass glided off, he saw the national insignia on the dorsal surface. But it wasn't the ancient Red Star of Russia, as he had naturally expected, but a depiction of the American flag.

It was an American ship. It was, in fact—it had to be—the

S.S. Van Dine.

The ship moved smoothly into the distance...then paused, as if it had become conscious of a mistake or of something left undone. It hung there, perhaps half a mile separating it from the other ship, its twin, which could only be the *Raskolnikov*... the portal of which had been left invitingly open. Minutes passed. A thin crescent appeared on the side of the *Van Dine*, widened, brightened into a full moon. He saw a manlike figure silhouetted against the glowing circle, a spread-eagled shape that filled the entire airlock, and behind it some dimly-glimpsed smaller figures. And, as he watched, he saw the larger figure shoot across the gap, as if propelled, and into the open airlock of the other ship with an hilarious accuracy. The bright portal of the *Van Dine* again dwindled and darkened. Its rockets flared. He felt a gentle tug, the faintest blush of heat, and the ship fell sunward.

The opening on the side of the *Raskolnikov* also shrank and vanished. The small lateral jets of front port and rear starboard flared and the great mass swung effortlessly about. It showed the sun its backside. There was a startling burst of light and the ship shot away with an acceleration no human being could have survived.

Silence. Dooley was alone. He looked about. He saw the igloo, dark and lonely, behind him. Saw the precarious ground of choppy rock and the terrible stars. But he didn't see the *Doyle*. The ship was nowhere in sight, and when he tried again—and then again—to reach it by the suit-radio, found that it was also not within earshot.

Could it be that the captain and crew of the *S.S. Van Dyne* had removed Oreste from the scene? If so, that would mean that he was now on his way to Earth in the company of Commissioner Watt, Senator Bailey, Ralph and, of course, Edith Neal. But... what could they have done with the *Doyle*? It was more likely that Oreste had decamped. But why? He remembered the suspicion that had sickened him on his way here: that the intelligent, conscientious, indispensable, friendly and likeable Oreste had also been subverted by Edith Neal. But no, that couldn't be true, could it? The thought was so ludicrous it was laughable. And yet...and yet he knew that half an hour ago he would have said the same of Ralph Phelps.

Well! This was an awkward situation. Awkward, because he had no means of transportation. Neal's clodhopper, squatting on the other side of the igloo, had been rendered useless by being stripped of its tanks and air-recycling equipment. And he had no access to Edith Neal's flyer, or, for that matter, even to the familiar *Christie*, because of the daily-changing security codes.

Awkward. But not life-threatening. He would simply go back inside the igloo and use the radio equipment there. It would do him no good to call Hap Lyles, because the only two vessels Vesta had, the *Doyle* and the *Christie*, were both here. But he could easily contact Eohippos, which was now close, and get help from the Russians by invoking Consul Gerasimov's name.

His hand had barely touched the outer rim of the entrance-tunnel when something glinted to his right. In the next second—in less than a second—he saw debris spewing to the left from the rear of the igloo: nondescript pieces of electrical equipment, plumbing, pots and pans, clothing, bedding and other furnishings. And, tumbling among them, considerably slowed by the impact, something he instinctively recognized. It was a helmet. He at first glancingly thought that Carl Neal's missing Westinghouse helmet had come home to roost—come home with a vengeance, punching a hole through the igloo and eviscerating it—but it was far more likely to be the Gorky helmet of the murdered Petra Wetjen. It was moving at too great a speed to have been flung away by hand—it must have been ejected from a ship just getting underway. All this he understood in a timeless moment. And in the next moment he saw a shudder go through the igloo and saw it collapse inward and downward, slowly, mournfully, like a deflated dirigible.

Dooley, in shock, found himself gripping the outer rim of the tunnel so hard his fingers hurt. He managed to let go and to push himself away. His feet trailed on the ground like weights attached to a balloon. He looked around again, saw what he had seen before, except that now the igloo, his place of refuge and means of rescue had been trashed...and felt himself trembling inside his suit. He tried to stop it, but, to his mortification, couldn't. He had been the hero of far more adventures than even Ralph knew about. His "cases" could have filled four or five books, not just one. He had faced down desperate men and had worked and fought his way through some dangerous situations with hardly a tremor...but now he couldn't control the shivering in his arms and legs, for now there was no chance of survival. And he found that he was breathing deeply—too deeply; he was breathing wastefully—for he knew that at best, his air couldn't last more than four or five hours.

Well, it looked as if this was it. The trembling gradually subsided...but, still, it looked as if this was it. His feeble suit radio couldn't possibly reach Vesta or even Eohippus. He would die a lonely, desperate, suffocating death on this piece of rock in the middle of nowhere.

He sighed and looked towards Indiana...and, again, a movement caught his eye. Almost directly in front of him a small ship was rising above the horizon of Albion. He greeted it even more joyfully than he would have greeted the rising sun on a glorious morning on Earth, and he made an involuntary bark of laughter when he heard Oreste's cheerful voice saying,

"I'm here, Chief."

CHAPTER THIRTEEN

And at last Dooley was back inside Vesta and sitting comfortably at the usual table in the familiar cafeteria with Heloise and Oreste. The fourth chair at the table was unoccupied. Dooley had glanced at it once or twice after sitting down, but that was all. He was surprised to find that the videomural had not been changed. The surf still whispered on the white beach, the ocean still heaved gently in the distance and the palm trees swayed in the Pacific or Caribbean breeze. But, he remembered, the murals were only changed once a week and he had been gone, unbelievably, less than a day.

Oreste was saying, "I was really startled when I saw that giant space-suited figure come out of the airlock of the *Raskolnikov* and go into the igloo"—he had been watching the scene through the telescope. "The size of the guy worried me a little. So I took a chance and radioed the Captain of the *S.S. Van Dine* and he told me something that *really* worried me—and that is that Petra Wetjen was only four feet eleven inches tall.

"Since I couldn't raise you on the radio and he couldn't contact the Senator, we decided on the little stratagem of switching the ships. My idea, originally. If there was something wrong inside the igloo, it might mean a way out. And, if there wasn't, if everything was okay...well, it would be harmless enough. Fortunately, it paid off.

"I kept a low profile because I didn't want the Giant to know I was nearby. If he had learned you had an ally on the scene— and of course you hadn't mentioned my presence when the two of you were talking by radio earlier—he might have become alarmed and alert to danger and the substitution of the ships wouldn't have worked. To escape his notice as much as possible, I snuck the *Doyle* around to the other side of Albion...although I'm afraid that mass of nickel and iron kept us out of radio contact."

"No harm done," said Dooley, speaking around a bacon, lettuce and tomato sandwich. He had a shrewd suspicion that Oreste, after being unjustly placed on the list of suspects—it had of course been Ralph who had removed the helmet from the *Doyle*—hadn't been adverse to giving him a little scare. He added, as if the matter were hardly worth mentioning, "You showed initiative and resourcefulness."

He noticed that Heloise was quietly glowing. It was like a faint, mellow reflection of that infatuated radiance Ralph had shown; but she had good reason, he knew, to be pleased. She had not actually been the first to break the news—the Captain of the *S.S. Van Dine* had anticipated her—but the story she had been able to provide the Interplanetary News Service was far more detailed than the Captain's brief dispatch and had been broadcast all over Earth, with her byline. She would probably get a good piece of change from it too.

"You have to give the guy credit," said Dooley, referring to the Captain. "He acted according to both the letter and spirit of the law. After Ralph confessed to him, he radioed the information to Earth and took Bailey and the others into custody— even though Bailey is one of the owners of the yacht and so, in a sense, his boss, not to mention his being a powerful senator."

Heloise said, "But he declined to hand the culprits over to you?"

"I didn't try very hard to persuade him. We have nothing here resembling a court until the circuit judge comes around and that would have meant holding the four for a dangerous length of time. Earth is the best place for them. Any judgment here would just be appealed there, anyway."

"How did you know the chair was filled with Ganymedan

air?"

"It had to be, because we'd found it would be inflated to full size under the atmospheric pressure of Ganymede. Wetjen took the chair with him to the moon so that he would have something to sit on while conferring with the Ganymedans in their natural habitat. They sit on their tails, you know. Of course he took it along collapsed and inflated it there—that's the idea of inflatable chairs."

Dooley's chin wagged silently for a while. Then,

"The instant I saw the supposed Petra Wetjen, I knew, or all but knew, he was a Pug—a Ganymedan. That's what 'pug,' means," he explained to Oreste: "'Perfectly Ugly Gent.' But," he added for Heloise's benefit, "I won't use that word anymore. Anyway, I knew what he was but I was puzzled as to what he could have done with that kangaroo-like tail. Of course he had it stuffed into that enormous backpack, which probably also contained a refrigeration unit. To us, it was cool, even chilly, inside the igloo, but he would have died of heatstroke if he hadn't had some means of keeping his (forgive me, Heloise) tail cold. I have an idea that what he called 'the balmy breezes of Golgonooza' would have frozen...." He groped for a phrase, which Heloise supplied:

"...the balls off a polar bear."

"Thank you, Miss Jamison. Dose am de words I was looking for."

If so, he seemed to be looking for them on the horizon. Out there, distantly, the white sail of a boat was yawing gently in the waves. He watched it for a while, perhaps longing for Earth, then, following some unspoken association of ideas, said,

"So the Big Nowhere was once Somewhere, after all."

Heloise surprised him again by saying, "Everywhere is Somewhere, if love is there."

"Yes," said Dooley before taking another bite of his sandwich, "you must tell the Ganymedans that Golgonooza resides in their hearts, if they only knew it." But he remembered that look Edith Neal had turned about the igloo.

"You know," he went on after another moment, "if Ralph had got around to writing that book, it's just possible he could have found a connection between the three separate stories, after all. Have you noticed that the Keeper's idea of purging our four friends of their moral sicknesses bears a resemblance to the ideas of the Purgationists who kidnapped Izak Gerasimov? And 'The Rain of Terror'—Schleffin's sabotage, which caused tiny chunks of the Belt to hit the Earth—is like a replay in miniature of the Destruction of Golgonooza. I have no idea what it means... but it's curiously suggestive, isn't it? I rather liked our friend, the Keeper of the Vault, but I have an idea that some day the human race may be coming into direct conflict with the Simple Ganymedans. Not just yet, but some day. The Ganymedan year is far longer than ours—in fact, they seem to measure time in eons. Dealing with them," he said, with a casual glance at the young man and woman sitting with him, "will be the work of future generations."

Oreste nodded, as if in agreement. He said, "And then there are those mysterious Old Ones."

"Well, maybe they don't have to be taken all that seriously. Or, anyway, any more seriously than we take such things as the Garden of Eden and Noah's Ark and the Flood. Maybe they were invented to invest what really was just an accident with...well, with human meaning. On the other hand, they might be for real. For, where did the Ganymedans get such technology as they do have? And how did they get from Golgonooza to Ganymede? But if the Old Ones are lurking somewhere, I suspect they're lurking quite a distance off—a few light-years off, since we've never caught even the faintest glimpse of them."

For some minutes there were only eating noises: the sound of chewing, mostly from Dooley, and the occasional clink of fork against plate. And then, Heloise, still glowing:

"I have some news for you. I was going to save it for your Going Away Party tomorrow, but I just can't hold it in any longer. It came over the newsfax an hour ago. We need a new Commissioner here and a name has been proposed to the

Asteroid Regulatory Commission. Guess whose. It's someone sitting at this very table. And, no, I don't mean you, Oreste."

Dooley nodded. "I've heard. But don't count on it. I'm a little sick of Vesta just now and would like to stay Earthside for a while. I mean, I'd like to hang around even after the trial, perhaps forever. But it may be," he went on, thoughtfully dissecting his potato salad with his fork; "it may be that after a few months I'll get tired of dragging my two hundred and twenty pounds around in Earth gravity and will want nothing better than to come back here where I'll once again be 'light-footed, light-headed, and light-hearted'"—he was quoting a line from a song once popular in the Belt—"or, anyway, where I won't be tired all the time. If so, I'll accept the Commissionership, if the offer still holds good. And, in that case, you'll be in line for the Chief Inspectorship, Oreste. You're awfully young for the job, but... well, there's no one I'd rather see get it."

Oreste smiled, shrugged his shoulders. "There are two great sins in the world. One is impatience."

Dooley noted that Heloise did not ask, "What's the other?" but noted it only absent-mindedly, because he was preoccupied with something he wanted to say.

"If I do decide to come back, I may...well, I don't know for sure, but maybe...." He was having a little trouble getting the words out, even though his sandwich was now gone. "If I do decide to come back, I think I will look around on Earth for a wife to bring back with me." Two pairs of eyebrows, blond and brunette, were raised by this announcement. "And that means, Oreste," lifting his eyes to those of the young man and speaking in a tone in which jocosity and reproof were equally mingled; "that means that, with me out of the running, you'll have a clear field with Heloise."

Heloise and Oreste both exploded with laughter. They rocked back in their chairs. Oreste's light freckles vanished as the skin around them flushed with color.

Heloise said, "We're going to be married on our next Earthside vacation." She held up her left hand, spread the fingers, and he saw that a gold band encircled the ring finger, "I've been wearing this for the last week and you never noticed. A swell detective you are!"

ABOUT THE AUTHOR

ARTHUR JEAN COX has written many stories under many names, a few of which he thinks it best not to mention. Those he would gladly mention include "Say That He Still Lives!" and "The Spectacles of Jorge Luis Borges" (both as by Arthur Jean Cox), "Writers of the Purple Page" (as by John Thames Rokesmith), "A Prince of Snobs" (as by Arthur Pendennis), and "An Occurrence on the Mars-to-Earth Run #128, at Approximately 2400 Hours, 21 January 2038" (as by William Dean). He would also include in that favored category all the contents of this present volume, and, any and all future publications of his fiction by Borgo Press and/or Wildside Press.

www.ingramcontent.com/pod-product-compliance
Lightning Source LLC
Chambersburg PA
CBHW031403250626
47155CB00004B/1396

A COLLECTOR OF AMBROSES

Each of the stories here takes as its subject some aspect of popular fiction—mostly, fantasy and science fiction. The title story contemplates the uncanny fascination of collecting—as it must, for it is one in which three unscrupulous collectors encounter a Completist. Another, "The Boy in the Iron Mask" (which the author tells us was suggested by an incident in his own boyhood), touches upon what Jorge Luis Borges has identified as one of the four fundamental forms of fantasy, "the contamination of reality by dreams"—but it is also about the awakening of courage.

A third, "*The Slaves of Moxon* and Other Tales of Scientific Romance," embodies an irony: that a notion peculiar to science fiction—the suppose existence of parallel universes, with alternate histories—should be directed back upon science fiction itself. And there is also a *coda*, which is not to be overlooked: "A Reply to L. Ron Hubbard."

Four great tales of speculative fiction by a master storyteller.

Borgo Press Books by ARTHUR JEAN COX

The Asteroid Murder Case: A Science Fiction Mystery
A Collector of Ambroses and Other Rare Items

A COLLECTOR OF AMBROSES

AND OTHER RARE ITEMS

ARTHUR JEAN COX

THE BORGO PRESS

MMXI

A COLLECTOR OF AMBROSES

Copyright © 1971, 1975, 1994, 2011 by
Arthur Jean Cox

FIRST EDITION

Published by Wildside Press LLC

www.wildsidebooks.com

DEDICATION

For Douglas Menville,

Writer, Bibliographer, Friend

CONTENTS

ACKNOWLEDGMENTS

SEVERAL OF THESE STORIES WERE previously published as follows, and are reprinted (with minor editing, updating, and textual modifications) by permission of the author:

"A Collector of Ambroses" was first published in *The Magazine of Fantasy & Science Fiction*, September 1971. Copyright © 1971, 2011 by Arthur Jean Cox.

"The Boy in the Iron Mask" was first published in *The Magazine of Fantasy & Science Fiction*, November 1975. Copyright © 1975, 2011 by Arthur Jean Cox.

"*The Slaves of Moxon* and Other Tales of Scientific Romance" is published here for the first time. Copyright © 2011 by Arthur Jean Cox.

"A Reply to L. Ron Hubbard" was first published as a one-page flyer by Dean Walter "Redd" Boggs in 1994. Copyright © 1994, 2011 by Arthur Jean Cox.

A COLLECTOR
OF AMBROSES

The Ambrosia Bookstore, on a quiet side-street in Glendale, was the cleanest, neatest, best-lighted bookstore in the whole wide world. Its merchandise—and this might have surprised someone wandering in casually off the street—consisted almost entirely of old pulp magazines, comic books and comic strips, "Big Little Books," and movie posters. But so neatly was everything wrapped (in cellophane) and displayed that the word least likely to suggest itself to this casual wanderer would be the word "trash." No other word in the English language was so defied, so set at a distance; the immaculate shop was its very antonym. But if this visitor, possibly middle-aged and sour of face, and, moreover, abysmally ignorant of the livelier arts, was unimpressed by the crisp and crinkly setting and not intimidated by the poster of King Kong glowering down from the wall—if this visitor, on seeing a copy of the third issue of *Action Comics* proudly displayed in a glass case, had felt that word rising to his lips like a bubble of gas from his dyspeptic stomach, he would quickly have choked it down again on seeing the price tag ($200!) also displayed. And, looking around, he would have seen other things that would fill his soul with awe: comics for sale at prices that would deprive him of all power of laughter; and old science fiction magazines for which were asked amounts that might well have evoked their exclamatory titles—*Amazing! Startling! Astounding!*

What sort of person, he might wonder, paid such amounts?

Did anyone pay them? Well...there were customers in the shop, mostly, though not exclusively, boys and young men. He would hear none object to the prices, see none express astonishment. Watching and listening, not obtrusively but furtively and feeling rather like a spy, he would discover that many of the customers were known to each other and to the proprietors; that here was a society of sorts, a little world of gossip and of curious esoteric knowledge, of ambitions satisfied and aspirations thwarted. If he wished to know more, he could easily strike up a conversation with one of the browsers in the store, a young man, for instance, in horn-rimmed glasses and a black bow tie, artfully eliciting from him information about the owners, their names, ages, and so on. This young man would cheerfully answer the questions at first; but gradually becoming conscious of something peculiarly insistent in the stranger's manner he would study him curiously and then drift away among the counters. After which, our visitor would wander outside again and, standing on the sidewalk in the bright California sunshine, would look around as if to get his bearings and (Glendale being a small town) would very likely see an acquaintance—a senior citizen, say, loitering in a straw hat on the opposite side of the street—and would nod to him, as if in recognition, and then walk away, the neat little magazine store slowly fading from his memory like a dream. Stranger things have been known to happen.

But, behind him, the store itself would not fade away, but go quietly about its business. Or, quietly enough, making allowance for a rather large amount of chatter.

The Ambrosia Bookstore was presided over by a young couple named Ambrose. Bill and Coolanthe Ambrose. They were very much alike, so much so that they had more than once been mistaken for brother and sister. Both were blond, blue-eyed and delicate, with remarkably fresh complexions: they were, as someone had once said, Mint Copies. They even had the same last name. This might not have struck anyone as odd, inasmuch as they were married, but Mrs. Ambrose had been a Miss Ambrose and there had been for a time some sticky

business with the Registrar's Office back in Minneapolis (their native town) before they had managed to prove that they were not barred from obtaining a license by any traceable consanguinity.

Their marriage had not been blessed with issue (nor was such an issue in store) and yet they were not alone. Not only had an eager horde of collectors found the way to their door, but they had a faithful friend who was very particular in his attentions to them. He was so much in their confidence that he had free access even to the Back Room—that so mysterious, so wonderful, Back Room, upon the momentarily opened portal of which (opened to admit *him*) a hundred young fans and collectors had turned their wistful eyes. So Bill and Coolanthe were not surprised one Thursday afternoon when the store was otherwise quiet and deserted—the calm before the storm, Bill afterwards said—and they were puttering in the Back Room, to see a familiar figure come through the tinkling front door of the shop and present itself a moment later at the generously gaping entrance of that sanctum sanctorum.

"Greetings, Sid!" called out Bill, gaily. "Have you seen the Dweller in the Closet lately? Would he like to visit again? Is he prepared to pay rent?"

This was a reference to the famous Closet Incident, which could never be mentioned too often and which ordinarily couldn't fail to evoke a smile from Sidney. The Dweller in the Closet had been Jack McMinion. Jack was a writer in a modest way, with a dozen or so stories scattered through the various science fiction and fantasy magazines. These had never been collected in book form, and he was fond of saying that few things were so rare as a complete Jack McMinion. The Ambroses didn't really much care about that. What had brought Jack to their attention was that he had a closet, a Magic Closet, as he humorously and affectionately had termed it, from which he had one day extracted and offered for sale some fifteen years' accumulation of old magazines and books. This they couldn't overlook. For, curiously enough, the Ambroses were fighting a

far-flung, many-sided war against all other dealers in the field. Their conversation consisted of a running commentary on the eccentricities and suspect practices of all dealers other than the Ambroses; and they had a habit of seizing upon one particular person, electing him Enemy of the Month, and concentrating all their scorn upon him until they had demolished him to their own satisfaction. They devoted the Merry Month of May to this new "competitor," Jack McMinion.

The Ambroses called Jack one day early in May and. asked him to stop by. They had something to discuss with him that might be to his interest. He came in and they greeted him graciously, even effusively. Bill draped his arm about Jack's shoulder and invited him into the Back Room, a rare privilege. Jack was touched and gratified; he felt that he had misjudged the Ambroses...for he had heard stories. They said with a smile that they too had a Magic Closet, the one right here. Wouldn't he step in and examine the rarities it contained while they attended to some urgent business in the shop? He could take his time; they were in no hurry. Jack stepped in—and Sidney, who had held himself in abeyance behind a book case, glided forth and clapped the door shut and locked it. The Ambroses then walked into the shop, which was crowded, it being Saturday afternoon, and announced that they had just had "the good fortune to acquire a complete Jack McMinion."

Coolanthe released Jack after an indefinite period of time. She says ten minutes; he says half an hour. Jack was rather heated and flustered. He indignantly used the phrase "unlawful confinement," but the Ambroses merely laughed, saying that after all it had just been an accident—the door had swung to and the latch had caught. He couldn't prove otherwise, could he? And he hadn't been harmed, had he? And wasn't he being just a wee bit humorless? This last was a point that they developed extensively in print and very effectively. Sidney disarmed criticism further by writing a sonnet in Lovecraft's manner, "The Dweller in the Closet," which was mimeographed in the pages of *Serendipity*, a publication for collectors, and much admired.

"Would he like to lease or buy?" persisted Bill. "Does he know what property taxes are like these days?"

But this time his humorous sally failed to get a grin from Sidney. Sidney was grave. Sidney was unusually grave as he came forward and wordlessly handed Bill what appeared to be a piece of a page torn from a newspaper.

"What's this? A dealer?...advertising in a neighborhood throwaway? Must be some kind of...."

Bill was probably going to say "junkshop," a favorite phrase of contempt with him, but he was struck speechless in an instant. He stared.

"'The Winter 1928 *Amazing Stories Quarterly*, 25¢' 25¢? That must be a misprint for $250. And what's this? 'First issue of *Weird Tales*, 25¢.' 'Various issues of *Superman*, *Batman*, etc., 1939, 1940, 1941...10¢ each!' This guy must be insane! Who the hell is he, anyway?"

He glanced at the top of the column, in which the name of the dealer was printed in block letters.

"A. I. Sorbma? Never heard of him. Wait a minute! Wait! Wait...."

The knowing Sidney waited.

"*A. I. Sorbma....*" Bill's scalp crawled, visibly. "*Why—that's 'Ambrosia' spelled backwards!*"

Coolanthe hung on Bill's shoulder, mouth open, eyes wide. "It's probably some trick of that Flowers creep," she said: Flowers being the name of their chief competitor.

"I'll bet there's no such place even," said her husband. "Only, there's an address given...in Burbank, not far from here. No phone number. Hmmm, there's a mystery here," mused Bill, fingering his hairless chin. "I think Coo and me should take a run over there and look at the place and maybe have a few words with this fellow, if he's for real. Why don't you come along, Sid? You can lend moral support."

"That's why I'm here," said their friend.

This friend's name was Sidney Fergus.

* * * * * * *

Sidney was not very pleasing to look at. He had a swarthy complexion, further darkened by a perpetual five o'clock shadow, large eyes, a crooked mouth and, somehow, although he was barely thirty—the Ambroses of course thought "poor old Sid" was over the hill—a battered and weathered look. In other words, he was definitely not a Mint Copy; but, despite this, he possessed a degree of charm that had made him many friends and admirers. He had a way of bestowing his full attention upon whomever he was speaking to, which, combined with a grave and yet whimsical courtesy, rendered him irresistible. And he had also something that particularly intrigued the ladies: a touch of iron in his very suavity, a glowing little spark that looked as if it might, under some circumstances, flame into violence.

Sidney's relationship with the Ambroses was puzzling to some of the fellows in the front room, but others had rightly made out that it was of a half-intimate, half-business nature. He was useful to them in various ways and they rewarded him with small items from their stock, either at discount prices or as outright gifts. He had an insatiable appetite for fantasy, particularly the more fanciful kind, but it was sometimes observed that he indulged this taste with a slight air of condescension, as if conscious of an inward superiority to such reading. Perhaps this was because he was more than a mere collector of old copies of *Weird Tales*. He had a serious literary interest. He was, by his own confession, the World's Foremost Authority on Ambrose Bierce.

Yes, *Ambrose* Bierce. One of the things that had most recommended him to the Ambroses when he first met them was his saying to them in his most charming manner that *he* was that collector of Ambroses mentioned by Charles Fort. Whereupon Bill explained to the blankly enquiring Coolanthe that Ambrose Bierce—

"The great writer Ambrose Bierce," amended Sidney.

—the great writer Ambrose Bierce had disappeared in Mexico in 1913 and that another man named Ambrose...Ambrose—

"Small," supplied Sidney.

—Ambrose Small had disappeared about the same time, and so the eccentric genius Charles Fort had theorized that somebody was collecting Ambroses.

Bill and Sidney were both very much amused by this, but Coolanthe didn't join in their laughter. Her brow was...not exactly furrowed, but touched with shadow.

"Coo's probably wondering," said Bill, "why anyone would want to collect Ambroses."

"Perhaps," speculated Sidney playfully, "he's tried collecting Joneses and found they won't do. Or maybe he collects Ambroses because nobody else does—it gives him a clear field and no competitors. Or maybe he's looking for the right one and simply gathers in any Ambroses he runs across in the hope of getting that one. Or, better yet, maybe he collects all Ambroses to cover up the fact that he's really just interested in one particular Ambrose—and perhaps, my dear, that one is *you*."

But the sunny beam he directed her way failed to dispel the shadow on Coo's brow; so Sidney, modulating his tone downward, said that of course such a notion as to why Ambrose Bierce had disappeared was not to be taken seriously. He himself knew something of the subject. He had looked into the matter. He had written a. book, a book that the Establishment press had not seen fit to publish, in which he presented irrefutable proof that Ambrose Bierce had not been shot by Pancho Villa, as some thought. No, that had been a cover story to deceive the dreaded *Federale*. In fact, hinted Sidney, his grey eye taking in both the Ambroses, Bierce had lived on for some time and had been, secretly, the mastermind and guiding spirit behind the Mexican Revolution, drawing upon his experiences in the American Civil War to lead the Mexican people to victory.

Bill was much edified by this, but Coolanthe was still puzzled. Sidney naturally supposed that she was pondering the plausibility of his statement, but what she finally brought out was:

"Do you think there really is such a thing as a 'great writer'?"

Sidney gazed upon her a moment or two, politely smiling, and then turned aside to Bill and to a new topic.

Sidney was certain that there was one great writer, at least. His admiration for his favorite was unbounded and unqualified. Rumor said (and Rumor was right for once) that he had quarreled brutally with his best friend when that friend had dared to assert that in his opinion Bierce was not of the first rank. "Not even," that friend had added (and Rumor, whose information was all second-hand, failed to quote this), "not even among fantasy writers." This was a remark for which Sidney had never forgiven Jack—for that friend had been, indeed, Jack McMinion. Jack had said more than that, though, much more.

"You will notice," said Jack, pacing back and forth in a green shirt as Sidney sat listening, "that every story by Bierce ends in the same way, with a blow on the head. Or its equivalent, you understand. It's almost as if he had a program. What he does is he takes up one by one in his short stories the various virtues and sentiments, such as patriotic courage, childish innocence, the faithful love of a sweetheart, and so on, and then administers to each that blow on the head which is, *he* thinks, the period to every sentence and the sum of every transaction. He admires courage and so he's rather wistful when he gives it the ol' knock on the block, like he does in 'A Son of the Gods,' but he gives it, nevertheless. What he's doing, of course, is debunking romance and sentiment, but he goes after bigger game than that. For instance, in 'Parker Adderson, Philosopher,' what he knocks down is philosophical detachment. And in 'Moxon's Master'— one of his better stories, by the way—he manages to identify intellectual excitement with chess playing and then gives it those same five knuckles on the skull—gives the abstract a taste of the concrete. Bierce would refute Bishop Berkley—or Beezlebub—not with his foot but with his fist."

Jack laughed a little at this, as if to deprecate his own eloquence. He glanced at Sidney...who smiled. He went on to say, as Sidney sat waiting with his fists on his knees, that

Bierce's relation to fantasy was peculiar and his reputation among fantasy readers rather curious. "Consider what I think is his most powerful story, 'An Occurrence at the Owl Creek Bridge'—you remember it, don't you, Sidney?"

Sidney, his eyes fixed unblinkingly on Jack, nodded his head, twice, slowly. He remembered it. It was the story of a civilian being hung by Union troops during the Civil War. He is dropped, a rope about his neck, from a bridge towards the river below. We see what occurs to him: The rope breaks and he plunges into the river unharmed; he works out of his bonds in the water, escapes from a hail of bullets by swimming downstream, makes it to shore and runs through, the woods to his house, sees his wife on the veranda, runs towards her, reaching out his arms, and..."there was a stunning blow at the back of his neck." He is hanged. All these "occurrences" were his wishful daydream as he dropped through the air to the end of the rope.

"Notice," said Jack, raising a finger, "that even the sensation of being hanged is described as a blow—if not exactly to the head. But my point is this: What story ever so desperately embodied the impulse to *fantasize*? And what story ever brought that impulse so abruptly and so brutally up short? And yet it is characteristic of Bierce's entire practice. He takes romance, sentiment, fancy, gives each just enough rope, and then...that sickening thud. It's as if he were saying that this is what everything comes to in the end, this blow on the head; and since it must all end that way, nothing is really real except it. Everything else is just pretense, vanity, words, idle show. He thinks the Good and the Beautiful are discredited because they must succumb at last to that fatal blow. It's a form of power worship, isn't it? He's siding with what is stronger and not with what is better. It's narrow. It's the reverse of generous. It's pro death. And when you come right down to it, it's anti the spirit of fantasy. I think that's something for you to think about Sidney," mused Jack, pausing speculatively before his friend, "that you, who like fantasy so much, should have placed this writer at the center of your imaginative life." Sidney smiled again, ever so

slightly.

Jack went .on to talk about the pedantry of Bierce's style, his harshness, and occasional brutality to family and friends, and even the phenomenal ugliness of his mistresses, all of which, he argued, was relevant to the discussion. Oh, he admitted that Bierce had his strengths as a writer and his virtues as a man, but he ended by comparing him to the gentle Nathaniel Hawthorne, much to Bierce's disadvantage. "In short," said Jack, who had spoken at some length, "I wouldn't trade one Nathaniel Hawthorne for a dozen Ambrose Bierces. That's putting it a little strongly, I know, but I think," he said, turning his innocent and mild gaze upon the waiting Sidney, "that the best way to give an opinion is to express what you feel as firmly as you can. Making all due distinctions, of course. Er...what do you think of all this, Sidney?"

And Sidney rose from where he sat and administered to Jack a blow on the head that felled him to the floor.

Their friendship was somewhat strained after this. They had been partners in a small publishing venture, to which Jack had supplied the capital, the management and the labor, and Sidney had supplied the genius. The venture came to an end and Jack was bankrupted because Sidney declined to pay his share of the costs, saying that he had never been a partner in any real sense (which was true enough). Jack felt he couldn't hold him to anything because they had had no written contract. "A hand-shake," Sidney had declared magnanimously at the time of the agreement, "is good enough for *me*." And indeed it was. Jack even came to believe in time that a handshake was entirely too good for Sidney.

So Jack was ruined. Reduced by necessity, he rummaged in his closet and brought out his science fiction and fantasy collec-tion and offered it for sale in the pages of *Serendipity*. The ad caught the eyes of Sidney and the Ambroses simultaneously and became the occasion for their alliance—for that little stack of paper Jack had offered to the public at a sacrifice had been large enough to excite the greed, envy and malice of the Ambroses.

Sidney supplied them with many little bits of information about their "competitor's" foibles and weaknesses and shared their laughter, a generous action that cemented his friendship with them and showed them the way in which he might be useful. He had far more wit than they and composed for them three or four laughable broadsides (such as "LET A HUNDRED FLOWERS BLOOM," in which he sent up a pyrotechnical display of puns on their chief rival's name) and which were published in the guise of advertisements for the Ambrosia Bookstore. In addition to his other talents, he had a happy knack of finding out people who had items or collections to sell (dirt cheap) or money to spend (for items that were not dirt cheap) and bringing them around to the store.

The Ambroses were not ungrateful for these attentions, A fitful stream of magazines, books and even small checks flowed, or trickled, from their hands to his; and he, in turn, was inspired to further efforts. He not only put at their service, such gifts as he had, but sometimes his moral support—as he was going to do in the present case of this mysterious dealer, Mr. A. I. Sorbma. Bill and Coo would make the frontal assault on that fellow, if he actually existed. It would be his job to bring up the flank—that's why he was being taken along. Sidney, loitering on the sidewalk as his new friends carefully locked up their shop, knew this as well as he knew that he had shamefully treated a former friend.

Not that he bothered to specifically mention either fact to himself.

* * * * * * *

"Sid, you'll have to sit up front with Coo and me. I've got the back seat filled." Sidney peered into the back of the Ambroses' old grey Plymouth and saw sprawling piles of comic books of the more prosaic kind, nothing that would interest him. "I don't care to bring such trash into the shop," said Bill. "They'll get a little frayed back there before I get around to dumping them on a junk dealer, but the creeps who buy that kind of crap won't

care."

They drove towards Burbank. It was a bright sunny day. The tree-shaded street stretched peacefully before them, the light glowing at its far end like a promise. "Have you heard Bierce's definition of a road?" asked Sidney, as they paused at an intersection. "It's 'a strip of land over which one travels from where it was futile to have been to where it is useless to go.'" He chuckled, but that was more or less out of old habit. He was not completely unconscious that on such a beautiful day there was something about this specimen of wisdom that rather grated on the ear.

"Honey!" shrilled Coo. "The light has changed."

But Bill's eyes were fixed on two young boys on the sidewalk diagonally across the intersection from them. "Do you see what I see? That kid has an early *Batman*. A *very* early *Batman*!" He stepped on the gas, S-swerved the car across the intersection and came to a squealing halt beside the two boys.

"Well, young man." said Bill, leaning his head out of the window with a most winning smile, "what are you doing with that funny book?"

The two boys, each about six years old, stared at this strange man, suspiciously. The freckled boy with the Snoopy sweater and the *Batman* said, "Selling it. It's mine."

"Of course it's yours, young man," said Bill, soothingly. "I'd like to buy it myself. I like funny books, I do. Here"—shifting his weight to reach into his pocket—"here's a dime for it."

"No. I want one million dollars for it."

Bill turned a disgusted face towards Coo and Sidney. "Has everybody gone crazy today? First, a guy who's giving them away...and now this! All right, kid—how about a quarter? I'll give you a quarter for that comic book."

The boy stuck out his lower lip, obstinately. "One. Million. Dollars."

Bill and Coo looked at each other. Both smiled slightly. "I'll tell you what I'm going to do for you, kid," said Bill, reaching into the back and picking up two comics at random.

"You see these two funny books? They're worth half a million dollars each." The child stared at the *Love Comics* and the *Bob Hope Comics*, seeming to find them suspect. "Now, two half-million dollar books are worth one whole million dollar book—right? Here, take them." He thrust them into the boy's right hand, deftly plucked the *Batman* from the other. "A deal's a deal, kid." And drove off, leaving behind a little boy in tears on the sidewalk.

"Ha, ha!" said Bill. "What a stupid brat! They ought to keep comic books out of the hands of children, anyway. They just abuse the privilege. Put that in the glove compartment, will you, Coo?"

Sidney glanced sideways at the faces of the Ambroses. Both wore the same slight, self-satisfied smile, as if they had just swallowed something particularly agreeable. Sidney was silent, wondering within himself whether A. I. Sorbma would be so easily dealt with as that six-year old boy.

He didn't have to wonder long, for they hadn't far to go. The address given in the clipping proved to be a short and narrow side street (that they came upon almost by chance) a mile or so from the NBC studios. It was paved with bricks and looked much older, incongruously older, than the surrounding streets. It had been originally some sort of private driveway, perhaps, and was now hardly more than an alley. At first, they saw nothing resembling a bookstore. One side of the narrow street, or alley, was completely taken up by a storage warehouse. Opposite, reading back from the corner, was a Sunland filling station, a disused garage, a boarded-up feed and grain store, a small white clapboard building with—that was it!—A. I. SORBMA painted in black letters over the door, and a fenced in vacant lot or yard.

Bill parked the car in the alley and they walked across the crumbling bricks to the shop front. Piled on a window seat or ledge before the one large window were several magazines and books, as if thrown there casually. They bent their necks and peered in through dirty, flyblown glass, saw several tables stacked and heaped with magazines in no apparent order, the

whole place very dark and obviously very dirty.

The Ambroses drew back. Their lips curled in unison. *"It's a junkshop!"*

But Sidney's eyes glittered. It was in just such a place as this, unknown to other collectors and run perhaps by some ignorant old man or woman, stacked with magazines and books emptied out of some forgotten cellar or attic where they had lain untouched for decades, that he might hope to find...oh, anything! *The Tarzan Twins* for a dime, *The Outsider* by Lovecraft for fifty cents, sundry issues of *Unknown Worlds* for a nickel each... or even that one wonderful thing, that nameless book or magazine, the existence of which he would learn only when he found it, so rare that no one had even heard of it and more glorious even than those specific titles for which he had haunted second-hand bookshops, Good Will and Salvation Army stores, and miscellaneous rummage sales for years, and which would be *the* treasure, *the* acquisition, never to be duplicated by anyone else in a lifetime of searching.

He straightened and turned away to the door, hoping his friends hadn't noted his excitement or prolonged scrutiny.

"We may as well go in...."

"It looks like it's deserted," said Coo. "There's no one inside."

But pinned to a half-drawn blind behind the dirty glass door was a scrap of paper on which was scrawled:

PLEASE STEP IN
—*The Spider* (10¢ ea.)

"Ten cents each!" cried Bill, outraged. "He's giving *The Spider* away too! That magazine's hot right now."

Sidney turned the knob and pushed. There was a drawn-out creaking, like the sound effect of an opening door on the old *Inner Sanctum* radio program. He stepped inside. Bill and Coo crowded in behind him and closed the door. They stood looking about. The place was dark, except for that portion of the afternoon sun reflected from the white-washed wall of the warehouse

opposite—so that even its sunlight was second-hand. But it was enough to strike from the covers of the magazines stacked in the shadowy interior murky little patches of color, like the gleams from riches heaped in a pirate's cave. They listened. Silence. Coo turned her head and sneezed, and the dust went flying from the table beside her, disclosing the covers of old *Science Wonder Stories*, remarkably fresh and un-faded under their mantle of dust.

There was, curiously enough, an answering sneeze...from somewhere offstage. Sidney had for a moment the oddest impression that it was mocking and derisive.

Some shabby drapes at the back of the shop parted and an old man came into view, summoned either by Coo's sneeze or by the creaking of the door. Old? He was terribly old. Also terribly thin, completely bald, short, stooped and potbellied. He was wearing baggy pants held up by suspenders, a tweed vest over a grey flannel shirt, and spectacles of a very antique design (but this last was the only modern touch about him).

The gnome came forward, "May I help you?" Sidney was surprised and even embarrassed to see something very like his own collector's avidity mirrored in the gnome's face. It was, he decided, an eagerness painfully restrained, as if the old man were desperately hungry for customers but afraid of frightening them away by the nakedness of his desire. "I have," said this individual, "old books, magazines and comics, first editions and back numbers. As you can see," he added, making a whimsical little bob, "I'm quite a back number myself."

"We're collectors," said Bill in a suave, modulated drawl, "of old magazines and comic books, don't you know, and we're interested in seeing what you have, Mr....Mr. Sorbma?"

"Yes, I am Mr. Sorbma."

"Mr. A. I. Sorbma, I believe," said Bill, taking the fragment of newspaper Sidney had given him from his pocket and unfolding it.

"Correct," said the old man, looking upon Bill and the clipping with a dreadful suspense, as if Bill were a lawyer in

search of a long-lost heir and that heir was..."Ambrose Ichabod Sorbma."

"Ambrose?" Bill raised an eyebrow. "Our name is Ambrose."

"You don't say!" cried the old man, falling back and flinging up his withered hands—a gesture such as an actor on the Victorian stage might have used to express extreme astonishment. "All three of you—?"

"No, no. The lady and I are Mr. and Mrs. Ambrose. The other gentleman is our friend, Mr. Sidney Ferguss."

"And I," said Coo, with a saucy toss of her head, "was a Miss Ambrose before I married Bill and became Mrs. Ambrose."

"Then, my dear," said the ancient one, his eyes glittering behind his thick spectacles, "you are double-dyed in Ambrosiana."

"But, you know, Mr. Ambrose Ichabod Sorbma," went on Bill, "there is something even more amazing than that. We have a bookstore, Mrs. Ambrose and I...."

"A fellow laborer in the dusty vineyard!" cried the old man, clasping his hands.

"...and do you know the name of our bookstore?"

"No. Pray tell me the name of your establishment."

"Ambrosia," said Bill, leaning close and leering significantly, "The Ambrosia Bookstore."

"A clever name," said Sorbma, cocking his head thoughtfully to one side. "Ambrose...Ambrosia; ambrosia being the food of the gods, conferring immortality. Very clever. But 'amazing'? Nooo...I wouldn't say it was amazing."

"I didn't mean that! What's amazing is this: A. I. Sorbma is Ambrosia spelled backwards."

"No!" The old man repeated his former action of falling back and flinging up his hands—but this time the gesture was accompanied by a rapid little dance, a gleeful (and rather unexpected) soft-shoe shuffle. "What a coincidence!"

"You said it!" sneered Bill. "A bit too much of a coincidence, if you ask me. You don't know a man named Flowers, do you?"

"Flowers...Flowers?" Sorbma rubbed his chin. "Knew a man

named Rose back in '39. Archibald Michael Bassett Rose. Not that it matters."

"How about McMinion?" put in Sidney, absently, his gaze loitering about the littered tables. "Jack McMinion."

Sorbma turned his spectacles upon him; the whites of his eyes seemed to fill the lenses. "I believe, sir, that *you* are not an Ambrose? No? Neither first nor last name? I see." And he turned away, as Sidney might have turned from a damaged copy of a title he already had.

Sidney studied him. The resentment he felt at this snub was swallowed up, after a moment, by his consciousness that there was something not altogether unimpressive about Ambrose Ichabod Sorbma. The old fellow was small, ugly and very shabbily dressed—his suspenders didn't prevent his underwear (boxer shorts, with a *fleur-de-lis* pattern) from showing above the trouser line on the left side—but he possessed...what would it be called in a pulp magazine story? A murky glow? No—an aura. Yes, an aura of indefinable power, like that of the High Lama in *Lost Horizon*. That painful, trembling eagerness had passed and the old man was now simply, overwhelmingly confident of himself. More than that, he was elated, he was arrogant. He breathed, however dustily, an air of triumph. He was like a man on drugs, and perhaps could even be dangerous if he had a mind to be.

Sidney was both amazed and amused by this conclusion. What was equally amazing, though not nearly so amusing, was that his two friends were completely unconscious of, or unimpressed with, the old man's "aura of indefinable power," that is, with his hopped-up recklessness. Their bland faces expressed an innocence that he might have found frightening if Sorbma had been more immediately and unmistakably threatening. Even as it was, a current of alarm tingled through him—rather pleasantly, really, for it gave a slight piquancy to the situation. It was a good thing, thought Sidney, raising his hand to scratch his nose and watching the three others with a satiric speculation from behind that cover; it was a good thing he had come along.

Bill and Coo might need more than his moral support before this interview was over. They might need his strong right arm.

"Speaking man to man," said the male half of the Ambroses, jocosely, "let me tell you that you can't go on selling things at the prices you've advertised. It's not good for Trade. How much, for instance," turning to the table closest to hand, "are you asking for these 1940 and '41 *Astonishings*?"

"Cover price. Five cents each."

"Five cents each!"

"Too much?"

"Too much!"

"Well," said Sorbma, not so much, expressing as panto-miming a grudging decision, "I'll tell you what I'm going to do. I'll let you have them for two-for-a-nickel. But, mind you, I can't get any lower than that."

"*Indeed—you—can't*," agreed Coo, with withering sarcasm.

"I would, like to know," mused Bill, regarding the shopkeeper with a watchful speculative faintly-smiling contempt, "just who put you up to this. Frank Flowers? The Micawber Bookstore? Or Jack McMinion?"

"Those names again," sighed the old man. "Sir and madam, I'm not interested in your playmates, neither in your little friends or your little enemies. I'm in business for myself. There is no one," he said, casting a glance back over his left shoulder, "behind me."

"You look to me like an intelligent old man," said Bill, his eyebrows giving the lie to his words, "and maybe we can make you a better deal than they have."

Sorbma sighed again, in exaggeration. "Sir, I am not open to any deals, except one. You can buy anything—or everything— in the shop at the asked-for prices."

Bill caught at this. "Everything, you say? Well," looking around, "that shouldn't come to much. But if we bought every-thing, you'd be out of business, wouldn't you?"

"Not at all. There's much more where this came from."

"I'll bet there is!" sneered Bill. "I've got an eye for such things

and I notice you've got one of everything here, but *only* one of everything. And I know what that means. You've got hold of somebody's Life-Time Collection"—he visibly capitalized the words: he had gotten hold of one or two Life-Time Collections himself, to his immense gratification—"and you're peddling it in this dingy hole. Since you obviously don't even know the value of the stuff, the collection was probably stolen. I wouldn't be surprised if it was. You just don't see that many Life-Times."

Whereupon Ambrose Ichabod Sorbma threw back his head, revealing unsightly wattles, and crowed. It was both a laugh and a shameless exulting shout. Never had Sidney heard such a gleeful outpouring of triumph, such a cock-a-doodle-doo of victory, as came from the throat of that old bird! This spontaneous cry lasted about half a minute and was brought to a close only by its author stamping four times, very hard, on the floor, as if nothing else could possibly give expression and therefore relief to his exultation and, perhaps also, to his sense of the ludicrous. It was succeeded by a moment of silence...broken by Bill:

"What the Devil does the old fart mean!"

"I think," suggested Sidney, "that Mr Sorbma is amused by a private joke. Something about his own age, perhaps,"

Bill was at first blank. Then, picking up on this: "Yes, I don't doubt he's seen several life-times of that sort. He looks like he's outlived the Class of '48."

And Coo made a remark about "age feeding on youth," that was possibly even more apt than she thought, though in a different way: for Sidney's mind flashed back, unbidden, to that little boy left crying on the sidewalk...and the expression on her face, and on Bill's, as they drove off. Sorbma himself seemed much taken by the remark. He leaned towards Coo and, rolling his eyes to express the keenest relish, ostentatiously licked his chops.

"Ugh," said Bill. Adding, as a *non sequitur*, "These things can be traced, you know. I can find out where this stuff was stolen from and, if you don't return it yourself voluntarily, I'll take the matter up with the police."

Sidney wondered at Bill. He obviously thought that this scrawny old man was simply some harmless and helpless scrap of humanity—someone who couldn't fight back. Bill had his nerve, of course, but the nerve wasn't connected to any muscle. If he should see that Sorbma was capable of attacking him physically, he would moderate his tone quickly enough. Sidney was pretty sure of that, for he well remembered the manner in which Bill had declined an offer by Jack to punch him in the nose. But, just now, his friend didn't see anything. As for the scrawny old man, he regarded the young man with an amused and delighted absorption, as if here were a rare specimen indeed.

"I think we've wasted enough time on you," said the rare specimen. "You'll be hearing from us. Come, Dear. Come, Sid."

"Dear" was quite ready to go, but Sid couldn't wrench himself away. Here, on this table, were a stack of Gernsback *Amazings*; on the next table were *Astoundings* of the Tremaine period; and over there, most wonderful of all, some *Weird Tales* of the '30s, with glowing sensuous covers by Margaret Brundage.

"No, Bill," he said, "I think I'll stay and look around. I see some things here I might want to buy."

The proprietors of the Ambrosia Bookstore stared at him. "But we're leaving...."

"Yes, I understand. Don't worry about me. I can make my way home all right. There's a bus line two or three blocks from here, I think. I'll drop around in the morning."

The Ambroses exchanged a look that plainly said, "We should have known."

To which Bill added, aloud: "Don't bother dropping around in the morning. You can either come with us now, or stay away altogether. We don't like a traitor."

"A traitor? Oh, come now, Bill, isn't that a trifle melodramatic? I just want to buy a few magazines."

"Stolen property?"

"You don't know that. I see no reason to call *Mr.* Sorbma a thief."

"Mr Sorbma?"

"Yes, Bill. You repeat it, I repeat it: *Mr.* Sorbma."

The subject of this exchange said nothing...but his eyes danced.

Coo, as if long pent up, burst out with: "So you think you've found someone better than us to milk, do you? We knew all along what you were really after. You'd sell your best friend down the river for a 1932 *Weird Tales*."

Bill grinned satirically. "How's Jack these days?"

Sidney was stung. It was outrageously unfair that they, of all people, should present the matter in that light. After all, if he had sold anyone down the river, who was it who had done the buying? He was stung; but he had something in reserve too. Jack had once made some remarks to him that he had pooh-poohed at the time but which, somehow, he had never forgotten. He now pointed out to the Ambroses how much that accusatory stance they showed towards all other dealers in their field resembled the hatred so many small shop-keepers and marginal businessmen felt towards the Jews. It was based, he said, on the same mechanism of projection, the same habit of aggressiveness against others for faults that might be charged against oneself. "Ask yourselves why you—who are, when you come right down to it, essentially retailers of old paper products—ask yourselves why you should be so fond of using words like 'trash' and 'junk-shop'? Ask yourselves why you are so quick to accuse other dealers, like Mr. Sorbma here, of dishonesty. Ask yourself—"

"Why should we put up with this? Come, Coo, let's go."

Bill backed to the door, smiling contemptuously, his eyes playing between Sidney and the old man. He reached back for the door-knob...and groped. "What the...?" Looking back: "The damned door has no knob!"

"Ah! Yes!" cried Sorbma, mincing forward. "Meant to mention that. The door can't be opened from the inside. No knob and the latch always catches. Must have that fixed some day."

"How do we get out?" demanded Coo.

"By the back way. Come. Despite your uncouth remarks, I, one of nature's gentlemen, am all affability."

The two glanced at each other, disgustedly, but prepared to follow him. Not, however, before Bill got in a parting shot at Sidney. "Are you going to leave this fellow here unwatched? I never leave a collector alone in *my* shop."

"Ahh," said Mr. Sorbma, "I fully trust Mr. Non-Ambrose. And, besides, there's only the one way out. Look around, sir," said he, making a bow to Sidney, "until I return. I have quite a few treasures here, if you know such when you see them. I make a specialty of first issues and first editions and that should interest you: for, unless I am much mistaken, you are always on the look-out for Number One."

Sidney tried to show how lightly and easily he deflected this dart by returning the bow and asking drolly, "Have you any Ambrose Bierce?"

He immediately felt this to be a very stupid response. Sorbma cast a quick, a very shrewd, glance at his face, as if supposing his archness to hide some other meaning. Then, seeing that it did not: "Why, yes, sir. In fact," throwing a similar archness, mockingly, into his own manner, "I have a complete Ambrose Bierce." Sidney was instantly reminded of "the complete Jack McMinion" of the Closet Incident and his left eye, before he could quite check the impulse, flashed his amusement in the direction of the Ambroses, where it met with two unreflecting surfaces. Yes, of course.... These little jokes, that had been the chief delight of their intercourse, were not to be shared with them now. No, never again....

"Back this way, Mr. Ambrose and Miss-Mrs. Double-Ambrose. Step into my parlor." And Sorbma, with, a hospitable grin, held aside the dusty shop-curtain, which was not un-patronized by spiders, judging by the strands of dry spittle that drooled from the top of the frame. Sidney glimpsed a dark area beyond, relieved by a pale rectangle that he took to be a door. "My modest sitting room," explained Sorbma. "Admittedly, it's not much. But wait until you see my kitchen! Ah, there are

people who can't tear themselves away from my kitchen!"

The curtain drooped back into place and the three were gone from Sidney's sight as he turned, both eagerly and deliberately to the tables of magazines. To hell with Bill and Coo! He wouldn't so much as look up as they drove past the window. He heard his former friends and the shop-keeper go down some steps, still talking, heard their words chopped off by the sudden closing of a door—with a sound as sharp and final as the drop of a guillotine-blade.

* * * * * * *

He was alone. Alone with treasures that he *would* know when he saw them...and he saw them all around. His hands actually trembled as he fanned through the *Weird Tales*. There seemed to be a complete set here. It took him some time to realize that, because the copies were so sloppily piled and mixed up...and yet each copy seemed to be in Good-to-Mint Condition. How much was Sorbma asking for them? Twenty-five cents each? He checked his wallet and right hip pocket. $10.38. Hardly enough to buy them all. Perhaps he could gull Sorbma into accepting a check? He cast a brief side glance in that direction as he browsed through the Tremaine and Campbell *Astoundings* on another table, but somehow it didn't seem to be a feasible idea. Strange old man. He had such a penetrating glance. What did he mean when he said—

Hello! What's this? Copies of *Strange Tales*. And *Famous Fantastic Mysteries*! And a complete set of *Unknown Worlds*! Good God, he had to have them all! But how could he buy them all? Was there—he shot a wild glance at the closed door—any other way? It didn't seem so.

And so far he had fluttered only over the tables. There were shelves too. Those nearest him, on the right hand wall (as he faced towards the back of the shop) were inlaid with countless magazines. There were long yellowed rifts from the Golden Age of Munsey, whole fleets of *Argosy*, a run of *The Spider* (10¢

each), and six feet of *Doc Savage* followed by a lengthy stretch of *The Shadow*. Such were the riches offered him that, overwhelmed, his eye negligently dismissed the other magazines he saw there and turned to the shelves on the opposite side of the room, which were filled with hundreds of books. He moved across the room, towards them...paused, peered.

Long moments passed as he tried, almost vainly at first, to take in the titles. Was he dreaming? Here was the fantasy library of...his fantasies. He had often imagined the thrill of finding some one book such as this copy of *The Outsider* by Lovecraft (marked, as he found on opening it, 50¢ on the flyleaf: he somehow had known it would be). But to find not only that but everything else he had ever wanted was really too much to take in. It was almost disturbing. Beneath his mounting excitement was an undercurrent of something very like anxiety. But the excitement mounted.

Here was the finest Lovecraft collection he had ever seen, but there was much else besides Lovecraft. There were books by Dunsany, Blackwood, Machen, Le Fanu, Merritt, Chambers, Cabell, James, Bulwer-Lytton, and Poe—the Honor Roll of Fantasy. And here was an 1897 copy of *Dracula* by Ambr... that is, by Bram, derived from Abraham...Bram Stoker. A first edition, he supposed. Inside the front cover was a personal bookplate: *Ex Libris* A. Small. A. Small? A bell rang somewhere, distantly.

His eye was caught by some *Oz* volumes on the bottom shelf and it occurred to him that that might be the children's shelf and, if so, it was where he would find the infinitely rare *Tarzan Twins*. It was. It was marked—really, this was too much!—10¢ on the flyleaf. He didn't put this one back onto the shelf but laid it aside, under one of the tables, as being claimed. It was the first time he had allowed that laying-aside reflex of the book-collector to express itself, his natural instincts having been swamped hitherto by the wealth of what was offered him. He noted, while he was down there, that there were not only several fine editions of the *Alice* books but a good many books about

King Arthur and Merlin, some of them far too old and too heavy to be of much interest or use to children.

And there was more by the author of *The Tarzan Twins*. The second shelf swarmed with the Primal Horde, the bound magazine serials and first editions of Burroughs novels. The third shelf was given over to science fiction, much of it antedating Wells and Verne, including a few titles that he (he, Sidney Fergus!) had never so much as seen. Here, for instance, next to Wells' *The Food of the Gods* was *The Fixed Period* by Anthony Trollope. He knew generally what that one was about, though: a country in which anyone attaining the age of sixty was routinely put to death. Ha! That might not be a bad idea in some instances.

Having looked at the lowest shelves, he looked at the highest and saw that the top shelf supported a complete set of Wilson's *Noctes Ambrosianae*. That was a little out of place in such a library as this, perhaps...although its inclusion might be defended on the grounds that "imaginary dialogues" were fantasy. On the shelf just below were some titles he didn't recognize. He reached one down, the thought crossing his mind that maybe this was that fantasy so rare that he had never even heard of it. He was disappointed to find that it was merely a non-fiction account of a certain Archbishop Ambrose of sixteenth-century Moscow, who was barbarously slaughtered for sacrilege. Well, that didn't belong in this collection, surely, and neither did the books next to it, which seemed to be preoccupied with the doings of some saint of the early Church. It was a pity so much space was sacrificed to religion. But, he reflected wryly, it had its good side too. It meant he wouldn't have to buy everything in the store, after all.

What were these books here? Magnificent old volumes with marble covers and gilt lettering on the spines. Gothic novels, by the look of them. He ran his finger along the first half-dozen titles. Weren't these...? Yes, these were the Gothick novels so lightly mentioned by Jane Austen in *Northanger Abbey* and so long supposed to be fictitious. Wouldn't it be something if he showed up at the next monthly meeting of the Frankenstein

Fraternity with these under his arm? Well, it would be, if he could have gotten them under his arm, for they were mostly in three volumes each. And here was *The Monk* by Matthew Gregory Lewis, obviously the first edition. Odd...something tugged at his memory. It reminded him of something. Was it of *The Monk and the Hangman's Daughter* by.... Ah! Here was a book he liked much better, the marvelous *Melmoth the Wanderer* by Charles Robert Maturin. He pulled the first volume off the shelf, breaking a cobweb, and handled it lovingly. Melmoth, the Immortal Man, the Wanderer of the Earth! Was it a first edition? Perhaps not, but it was very old, for inside was an inscription: *"First Prize in English Composition Awarded to James Ambrose Cutting, December 1824."* James Ambrose Cutting? That was a name he had heard before in some connection. Something to do with...with photography? That's right. His old studies in that field blurred back into focus. Cutting was that nineteenth-century photographer who invented a method of making long-lasting pictures on glass, which he called Ambrotypes. Not after his middle name. No. The word was derived from the Greek *ambrotos*, meaning (*am*—not; *brotos*—mortal) immortal. But the inventor himself hadn't proved to be quite so long-lasting, had he? No, poor fellow, he had come to a bad end in an insane asylum. Not that that mattered at the moment.

Sidney put *Melmoth* back onto the shelf. A spider scuttled away. He stood staring at the backs of the books. Something was missing.... His eyes moved along the shelves, restlessly, and were snagged by a name. Of course! "...*How could I forget thee?*" Here, at the corner of the room, on the fourth shelf from the floor, was quite a little outcropping of Ambrose Bierce. Yes—the full twelve volumes of the *Collected Works*, the only books he had seen here that he already had in his own library. This must be "the complete Ambrose Bierce" the old man had boasted of. It would have been disappointing except that there were earlier Bierce printings as well, including a first edition of *In the Midst of Life*. Sidney opened that and discovered inside the front cover an inscription in ink: *"Ambrose Bierce, January*

1914." Bierce's autograph! This was a real find! But...1914? Bierce had disappeared in 1913. No news of him had been heard since that time....

The author of *The Secret Life of Ambrose Bierce* (for such was the title of Sidney's unpublished book) stared at the inscription. There was not the slightest doubt in his mind that the signature and date were in Bierce's handwriting. He had come into possession of several holographic letters by Bierce and would recognize that hand, with its characteristic cramped energy, anywhere. Sidney's own hand trembled. This was proof! Bierce had been alive as late as 1914, and perhaps later. He turned to the other books by Bierce. Perhaps there was more evidence here, evidence that would enable him to prove that Bierce had survived in Mexico for some time and was the secret genius and unsung hero of the Mexican Revolution. If he could prove that, if he could snatch from the backward abyss of time that credit which his hero so richly deserved, then his own name would be inextricably linked with Bierce's for all time to come. He opened the copy of *Can Such Things Be?* Something dropped from between its pages, which he snatched from mid-air with an alacrity that somewhat surprised himself. It was a photograph, an autumnal photograph, rather faded and sere. Not an ambrotype. It showed several figures, Mexican guerrillas or banditos, easily recognizable as such from countless old movies, clustered around an ancient touring-car. There were two figures in the foreground. The one on the right wore a wide sombrero and had a belt of cartridges strapped over each shoulder and crossing on his ample stomach: a stocky, mustachioed Mexicano—possibly, thought Sidney, Pancho Villa himself! This man, whoever he might be, faced the camera, teeth bared, but his body was half-turned to the right and his right leg was raised and his foot rested on the running-board of the old car...a romantic, if somewhat shabby, figure. But the other man! That lean, taut body, that cold hard pale gaze direct into the camera from beneath the straight, flat brim of the "cowboy hat," as if he were trying to stare the viewer out of countenance—that was Ambrose Bierce!

He, Sidney Fergus, now held in his hand an unpublished photograph of Ambrose Biercd! And one showing Bierce with Pancho Villa! He looked around the silent, deserted shop. He was alone. The dusty curtain at the back hung so motionless and heavy that it looked as if it hadn't been so much as stirred by a breath of air in thirty years. He could easily salvage this picture for his own purposes. Better that it should be in his collection than stuck here, unseen, in the pages of a book in a dusty shop. His hand flickered in the direction of his inside breast pocket... but the movement wasn't completed. For something had again snagged his attention.

He looked again at the picture. At a figure that was not so prominent as Villa (if indeed it was he) and Bierce. It was an old man, seated at the wheel of the ancient touring-car, one hand raised to his grinning mouth, his eyes twisted sideways towards the camera. It was, in fact, what's-his-name, the owner of this shop, Sorbma. So, Sorbma had once known Bierce personally! No wonder he'd had such a sharp reaction when Bierce's name was mentioned. Well, the old guy certainly hadn't changed much since that time, had he? Since that time...? Wait a minute. Something was wrong here. Let's see...Villa was killed in 1923, so this picture had to be that old at least and was probably some years older. Say it was made in 1915. That was something like ninety years ago. If Sorbma was now in his eighties, as he seemed to be, he wouldn't even have been born then. On the other hand, if he were in his eighties when the picture was taken, as he seemed to be, he would now be in his...*one-hundred and seventies*!

Sidney stared at the photograph with blank lapses of thought. Sorbma? One hundred and seventy years old? There seemed to be no way to take hold of such a notion. Perhaps the man in the picture was Sorbma's father? He tried to hold onto that possibility, that this was a picture of Ambrose Ichabod Sorbma, Sr., but couldn't. For he knew better: there were identical twins, but no such thing as an identical father and son. The mother's genetic contribution always showed itself.

The only other rational explanation was that it was a coincidence. Just two old guys who looked alike—and one of whom owned a picture taken of the other ninety years before!

It was curious and baffling—still another mystery connected with Ambrose Bierce. It would make an interesting half-page in his book on Bierce, when he got around to writing it.

A "mystery connected with Ambrose Bierce"...which reminded him, not unnaturally, of Jack's reservations concerning that man's greatness as a writer: that all his stories ended with "a blow to the head." Well, how else should they end? A story, after all, had to have a strong ending, and what stronger ending could a story have—that sudden blow, unexpected and catastrophic, which, striking down the hero himself, if need be, writes an irrevocable *finis* to the story? Who but a ninny would want a story to end any other way?

"Ha! Who but Jack McMinion!"

He was startled by the sound of his own voice—for he had made this last comment aloud. That sobered him, quieted him. In the reflective pause that followed, he saw, he couldn't help seeing, that he had pursued this little side path about Jack, to distract himself from something. He had been averting his gaze.

Yes...he stood staring now at the backs of the books on the shelf before him, actually seeing noting, but listening...listening for what? Not a sound was heard. Never had he been in so silent a place! He was touched by something, a tingling anticipation to which it was hard to give a name, but which was almost (not quite, but almost) like fear. But why should he be afraid? Wasn't he the man who had arisen from where he sat and struck Jack McMinion such a blow on the head that he felled him to the floor? He was made of stern stuff. He was easily a match for that old fellow.

Old fellow? What old fellow? Why...Ambrose Ichabod Sorbma, of course.

Now, what in the world did he mean by thinking something like that? "A match for that old fellow," indeed! Why should *he* be on his guard against Sorbma?

That old man was no threat to him. To...*him*? He wondered at the emphasis he had given the word. Why should the tottering, elated old derelict be a threat to anyone? He wasn't. And he certainly wasn't to Sidney Fergus, who was, after all—what was it Sorbma had called him? Oh, yes—"*Mr. Non-Ambrose!*"

He flinched away from the thought, or tried to flinch away, but it was too late. That small step he had taken, a step so natural and so easy to take, had brought him face to face with the very thing, the very recognition, he had been trying to avoid:

Sorbma was the Collector of Ambroses!

This dingy old man, lurking in this out-of-the-way-hole, was that being whose existence had been so shrewdly divined by Charles Fort.

"I think," said Fort playfully, "that someone is collecting Ambroses."

Someone was.

Ambrose Ichabod Sorbma.

Those disturbing impressions that had so lightly troubled Sidney's mind as he browsed, and which he had so lightly brushed away, came again into view...and converged.

"*Ex Libris A. Small.*" The name of the other man Fort had written about, the man who disappeared about the same time Bierce did, was Ambrose Small. Sorbma had at least one of his books here, perhaps more. But then the shelves were crowded with the name of Ambrose. James Ambrose Cutting, for instance. There, the middle name was the one of final importance. But apparently the name would do in any form, condition or accent. Such as Saint Ambrose, or Archbishop Ambrose of Moscow, or Ambrosio the Monk—no, he was a fictitious character, the hero of *The Monk*. Sorbma couldn't have had any real connection with him; it was just an incidental association. He was collecting Ambroses and was picking up along the way anything intimately associated with the name Ambrose... or Ambrosio...or Ambrosius? The original name of Merlin the Magician had been Ambrosius. But he was a fictitious character too, wasn't he? Surely. Who else—going on with the roll call—

was there?

Well, there was...

Bill and Coolanthe Ambrose!

But they had left! Hadn't they? Sidney cast an alarmed look at the inertly hanging drapery. How long had they been gone? He glanced at his wrist. Five o'clock. But that meant he had been browsing here for more than three hours! Good God, it had seemed more like thirty minutes. Surely, Bill and Coo were back home, in their shop—and had been for the last two and a half hours.

But where was Sorbma? Why was he himself still alone here?

His eye revolved of its own accord towards the front of the shop and the dirty, fly-specked window. The afternoon sun glared from the white-washed brick wall of the warehouse across the alley. He moved slowly in that direction, unseeingly past those piles of colorful magazines that such a short time before had seemed almost excruciatingly desirable; moved to the window and peered, rather anxiously, out. What he dreaded to see, he did see. He expected it and yet he was unable to suppress a little start and gasp of horror.

The Ambroses' old grey Plymouth was still parked down and across the alley. It was there. And that meant they were still in the shop. They had to be. They had been...detained...by Sorbma in the back.

That advertisement in the throwaway—why, why, why had he shown it to them? It had been an enticement, bait, to lure them to—this place. He hadn't even run across it by accident: he had found it in his mailbox. He had been made to act, unwittingly, as a Judas-goat. (It struck him suddenly, guiltily, that there was a dreadful appropriateness about that.) He glanced at the door beside him. How simply it had all been done! How easily the trap had been sprung! There had been no way out for the Ambroses, except through that back kitchen. He gave another start. "Back kitchen?" God, what a grisly picture that phrase abruptly brought before him. It was like a sudden splatter of blood.

He tried to steady himself by thinking the matter through. There was so much here that didn't make sense. Why should Sorbma want to collect Ambroses? Was he interested in all Ambroses? That hardly seemed likely. The name of Ambrose, all told, was Legion. He must be interested only in such Ambroses as had attained some notoriety, or who had somehow attracted his attention, or only in those who met certain specifications. Collectors were notoriously fastidious and often in ways inexplicable to the non-collector. But that didn't answer the essential question. Why should he want to collect any Ambroses, regardless of their qualifications?

Sidney's mind groped among the possibilities.

(1) He, Sorbma, is an Ambrose-hater. He once received some unforgivable, as he thinks, insult or injury from an Ambrose and now revenges himself against other Ambroses. (But he "collects" them—that certainly suggests ambivalent feelings.)

(2) He is himself an Ambrose. That is, he is a member of a family (in the sense that the Mafia is a family), or of a cult (say, of some alchemical cabal surviving from the Middle Ages, or from the days of Merlinus Ambrosius), or of a religious sect (those shelves devoted to religion hinted of such a possibility). Anyway, Sorbma is, or was, himself an Ambrose and he has caused other Ambroses to disappear, so that his own disappearance would not be attributed to disaffection. He has done this to deceive certain Watching Eyes or to elude Searchers—those of the family, fraternity, cult or sect, which didn't look with favor upon defectors or backsliders. This was a very tenuous speculation, but it was evident that Sorbma was hiding here, in this dark corner and under a concocted name, from Someone or Something.

(3) He needs Ambroses, not for themselves but because they are the raw material from which he distills...well, the Essence of Ambrose, which would be, naturally—*Ambrosia*! And what was Ambrosia? What did this terrible and terribly-old man say it was? "The food of the Gods, conferring immortality.

Sidney felt that with this last answer he had set his foot upon

the right path to the solution of the mystery. For this man, the grinning man of the old picture, must have done something to preserve—not his youthfulness, but his old age—into perpetuity. He must have taken something...and what should that life-prolonging something be called but "Ambrosia?" And how odd that this partaker of Ambrosia should be "interested" in Ambroses. There had to be a connection.

Looking ahead, he saw that this path converged easily with the two others. There was a small clearing, he found, where the three paths came together: one large enough for him to turn around in and get his bearings. That secret of immortality couldn't be Sorbma's, or Sorbma's alone. He hardly seemed to be a medical, chemical or alchemical genius. It must be the property of that secret and ancient society of immortals. Secret and ancient? Yes. Secret—for who had ever heard of it? And probably very ancient—people who knew they were immortals were not likely to have been born yesterday. Sorbma certainly wasn't. Anyway, the fact and method of immortality was probably the secret of that fraternity or cult, and Sorbma had fled, taking it with him. He would have to lie low, for, surely, any society with such a potent secret, one they didn't care to share with the rest of mankind—ay, there was the nub!—wouldn't allow drop-outs. The only egress from a Society of Immortals would be death.

What Sorbma needed, of course, was not Ambroses but simply people from whom to contrive his elixir. His favoring persons named Ambrose was simply his little joke, a bit of fancy footwork, a capering and a thumbing of the nose behind the broad back of that dread Fraternity, whose name was probably something like the Ambrosian Society or the Brotherhood of Ambroses. *He* would do something like that. He was a mirthful old man. He loved his japery. And why not? There was no logical reason why the collecting and feeding on Ambroses shouldn't be a thing of joy.

And it came to Sidney (as his gaze strayed around the shop) that perhaps Sorbma particularly relished collecting those

Ambroses who were themselves collectors...whenever he could find any. That would be the cream of the jest, perhaps; his idea of poetic justice. It would explain how he had come into possession of such a library as this. He must have gotten his hands at times on the collections as well as the collectors. If Sorbma did particularly covet collectors, then Bill and Coo would be naturals for him. He must have heard of them somehow, or have seen their advertisements. Everything, their family name, their position in the fantasy collecting world, even the name of their store, would render them ludicrously desirable.

Poor children, he wouldn't be able to resist them!

Children...that's what Sorbma had called them and that's what they were. They had been innocent. Their sanguine innocence had led them blindly into a trap laid and sprung by a being whose conception of evil overshadowed anything they might imagine. They had toddled forward, hand in hand, into the lowering gloom, like babes in the wood.

Sidney's eye again sought the old grey Plymouth. However uncertain his speculations might be in detail, there was nothing uncertain about that car. It sat stolidly and incontrovertibly there, its empty alarming presence confirming every fear.

The Ambroses had never left the shop.

He glanced again at the shop curtain. They were back there somewhere. Were they still alive? Maybe. Because Sorbma hadn't "remembered" him yet. He must still be...feeding...off them, or disposing of their bodies. But did he actually *eat* his victims? Consume chunks of their flesh? Drink their blood? That sounded like something from the worst sort of horror movie—and, after all, how could mere human flesh and blood confer immortality? No, he must do something else with them. Perhaps he absorbed—absorbed? *Sorbma*? No, that was too much! Perhaps he somehow fed on suffering? Perhaps he aroused his victims to paroxysms of fear, horror and loathing, and vampirishly ingested the floods of hormonal juices. Perhaps....

But there was no way to answer such questions. It was enough to know that the Ambroses might still be alive. Imagine

what they must be feeling if they were lying back there helpless, unable to cry out, but knowing that he was browsing a few yards away in the shop.

He had, suddenly, an almost sickening vision of water twisting down a dark drain: the lives of the Ambroses going down the drain.

He had to do something. He had to save them. He *would* save them—even if saving them meant only ending some unspeakable suffering.

And he had to do it now.

Moving with the stealth of a cat-burglar, he padded to the back of the shop. He pushed aside the curtain and peered into the chamber beyond. It was a room about the size of the shop. The left-hand side was obviously used only as a corridor. There was a stretch of bare and dusty flooring and a short flight of steps leading down to a door. The right-hand half was actually Sorbma's parlor or sitting-room. Its fittings were almost picturesquely shabby. There was an ancient desk, its roll top jammed open by accumulated papers, including copies of *Serendipity*, the familiar covers of which he could recognize from where he stood; a swivel chair, with one caster missing; a Morris chair, horribly decomposed and stinking and yet showing signs of recent usage—it was littered with the broken bits and crumbs from a half-empty cellophane package of crackers lying on one of the arms (which meant that Sorbma did not live on Ambroses alone); a small but once rich rug, trod under foot now for decades; a sideboard with a flaky iron tea kettle on a trivet; and, against the right-hand wall, beneath a papered-over window, an army cot—the most modern thing in the room and yet that probably a veteran of World War I.

So this was where Sorbma eked out a paltry eternity? But it was not...not his workshop. That must be on the other side of that sunken door there. That was the Back Kitchen, into which he had led Bill and Coo like lambs to the slaughter. And that's where *he* had to go.

He stood staring at the kitchen door, half in the shop and

half in the parlor, the curtain held aside with one hand. His watch ticked loudly. He cast a glance, almost involuntarily, back towards the shop window and the alley-way. His eyes fed hungrily on the light coming in through the window and the bottom un-shaded part of the door. He swayed. There crept into his brain a stealthy thought: "If I can escape, I can bring help and save the Ambroses that way, without going through that door."

Escape...? Yes. How it might be done occurs to him suddenly. It is easy, or, given desperation, easy enough. He runs from the spot he is at, past the tables of magazines, to the front of the shop. He snatches the shade and its roller from the door. He drapes the shade before him as a shield, and, with his left shoulder raised, his head lowered, his eyes closed, he runs three or four steps, strikes the glass door very hard. It shatters outward. He had meant only to break the glass and step through, but finds himself falling forward amid a shower of sharp fragments. His presence of mind does not desert him: he allows himself to fall, snatching his legs up and away from the bottom of the door, to avoid the standing shards of glass there. He strikes the bricks of the alley-way hard, taking the main force of the blow on his shoulder. But he is young, wiry and tough. He is hardly down than he is up again. He is a little shaken, his shoulder is bruised and there is a cut on his cheek, but he is otherwise unhurt. He takes to his feet, runs down the long alley, past the car of the ill-fated Ambroses—best to leave it where it is—and towards the open street beyond, towards light, air, safety, freedom. He *is* free, his heart pounding, his lungs expanding with joy, free of that horrible shop and its loathsome back rooms and....

There was a tingling at the back of his neck. A shudder went through his whole body, spreading from that point. With a voiceless cry, he twisted, slapped with his hand, brushed something from his neck. A spider. It lay on the floor of Sorbma's parlor like a knot of brown thread. It had let itself down, he, shuddering, saw, from the top of the door—a single silken strand still trailing from the curtain rod, its lower end wispily

touching the bare skin just above his collar. He shuddered again and, brushing at his neck, ducked out from under the doorway into the parlor, brutally crushing the corpse of the spider under his heel as he did so.

This small incident was peculiarly unnerving. But, despite it, and despite the means of escape that had occurred to him, he was still resolved to go through that door. Bill and Coo, in whatever condition, were still on the other side of it. It might not be the only way out of the shop, but it was the only way out of his uncertainty and suspense. And, besides, wasn't it what Ambrose Bierce would do?

The memory of that astonishing, that almost ferocious, courage that Bierce had shown in the Civil War, and, not only then, but all his life, reverted to him now with almost shocking force. Bierce, he knew, would flinch from nothing—and how could *he*, Sidney Fergus, not follow the example of his Hero?

He straightened himself and stepped towards the kitchen door.

He stood at the topmost of the four descending steps, which went down to a level about three feet below that of the floor on which he stood; stood staring at the door. It was a wooden door, divided into four panels and covered with a cream-colored enamel paint that was peeling and scabbing off. "Leprous," Lovecraft would have called it. It seemed to him a sinister door, sinister in its very shabbiness, reminding him somehow of a photograph he had once seen of an axe-murderer standing on the wooden porch of a dilapidated clap-board house. Nonsense, he told himself: it's just an ordinary door, no different from a thousand other doors. It wasn't, for instance, at all unlike that door he had clapped shut on Jack McMinion, imprisoning him in the closet while the Ambroses stepped into the shop and announced....

A shudder went through him. His hand reflexively slapped at his neck...but this time there was no spider, there.

For Sorbma had said, *"Yes...I have a complete Ambrose Bierce!"*

And that's what he had meant! That's what that look, so penetratingly, so arrogantly, shrewd, had meant! He actually had in his possession Ambrose Bierce himself. Not alive—no: preserved. There flashed before Sidney's vision a picture as from a Hammer horror film, with Sorbma as a mad doctor with row upon row of waxen corpses at his disposal—generations of Ambroses...with the most famous of all Ambroses as the star of the collection. If so, then when he looked into that grisly kitchen, he, Sidney Fergus, the World's foremost living authority, explicator, champion and collector of Ambrose Bierce, would gaze upon the countenance of his Author. He would—and here was a tantalizingly dreadful thought—he would be face to face with what would be, for him, the Ultimate Collectible: but one that was forbidden, taboo, unthinkable, obscene...and tantalizing. It would be the grotesque culmination of his personal life and surely one of the most bizarre incidents in the history of literature.

His wavering hand unconsciously touched the outside of the breast pocket where the photograph was hidden, very much as it might have touched his cheek if he had had a toothache. He was conscious of a pang like a foretaste of grief, a sense of emptiness and loss.

Bierce, he thought. Bierce, the man who was afraid of nothing, the man who not only had looked Death in the face but had shaken his hand, claiming him as a life-long companion, and who yet had managed to preserve his own fierce will and energy—that man had succumbed to *this*...this relic, this scarecrow, this grinning Grandfather Smallweed of a shopkeeper. The dragonfly had been caught in the web of the spider. But how was that possible? How could such a doddering old fool have defeated such a hard, cool and fearless a man as Ambrose Bierce? Could it be that Bierce, beneath that hard crust, had had some sort of weakness, some betraying touch of...well, call it fantasy.

Sidney himself liked fantasy, especially romantic fantasy. He was partial to *A Dreamer's Tales* by Lord Dunsany, the lush

reveries of Clark Ashton Smith, the glittering narratives of A. Merritt; his favorite Lovecraft story (although he had never mentioned it to anyone) was *The Dream Quest of Unknown Kadath*. But he felt this liking to be suspect. He indulged it in periodic debauches of reading, but he had a secret contempt for it. It was connected in his mind with everything that he thought was least admirable in himself, a tendency to dreaminess, romantic longing, softness; and so, after each such debauch, he would turn to its bracing opposite—chiefly, to Bierce. He admired Bierce because he was so tough-minded. But he knew, really, that there was more to it than that: there were hard-boiled writers of mystery and adventure whom he liked, but he had never made so much of them as he had of Bierce. He saw now that Jack hadn't been far off. What had attracted him to Bierce was that the targets of this man's aggressions had been idealism, romance, fancy and imagination, notions of honor and high ideals, a fascination with the exotic, the uncanny and the super-natural—the very stuff of romantic fantasy. But didn't Bierce's choice of these things as the objects of his wry contempt and cold anger unmistakably show his covert attraction to them?

He had always known the answer to that question, although it was one he had never posed to himself; but this was a moment for facing truths. He faced them now...and, as he did so, his thought took an effortless, intuitive, farther step and he saw that even if Bierce had managed to scour from his breast every trace of romance, idealism, and fantasy, there still remained his famous capacity for imaginative horror...and it must have been *that* that Sorbma had had to work upon. Bierce had supped on horror, and Sorbma—good God!—had supped on him!

But...if a man like that had succumbed to Sorbma, what chance would poor Bill and Coo have. None.

He would have to save them!

He started forward, put his foot on the topmost step. It groaned under his weight, loudly, as if he had accidentally stepped on a tortured man in a dungeon. The effect was so startling that he turned and ran several quick steps back to the curtain before

he caught himself. He turned, grimacing, deeply ashamed and cringing, as it were, from his own cowardice.

He faced the steps and the door again, bravely, and determined to face Sorbma as resolutely. He put his foot on the top step. It groaned, perhaps as loudly as before, but this time he kept his head and his footing. Sorbma must not have heard it. He was so deeply absorbed, it might be, in what he was doing that he could be roused by no sound or disturbance. The second step, which groaned or creaked at a lower pitch. The third, which groaned in bass. He was going down the scale. And then the solid floor, the blessedly silent, solid floor. He breathed a sigh of relief....

...and stiffened, froze: for from behind the door came a high-pitched scream.

Followed by another.

And another.

Sidney felt the blood draining cold from his face. He hadn't known that Coo could scream like that. Or that Bill could scream like that—for it could be either. Or both. And what screams! They were cries of fear, but not of fear only. They were shrieks of despair, of outraged protest, of insupportable horror.

To the rescue! His strong right arm was needed. Now was the moment to push open the door, dash in and fall upon Sorbma, taking him by surprise. But, like a dreamer in a nightmare, he was unable to move. His knees had turned to jelly. They wobbled. He remained standing, but in the same spot; to take a step would be to risk pitching forward on his face against the door.

The screams ceased as suddenly as they had begun. They were succeeded by a sound, low and faint, but distinctly recognizable as a chuckle. That sound fell on his ears as the most diabolical they had ever heard, following as it did on those screams. It was a chuckle, fat and self-satisfied, of someone gloating...gloating over a victim, growing stronger on someone else's suffering. It made his blood run cold again, but in the opposite direction. His legs steadied themselves. That chuckle was intolerable. Anger

checked his fear and made it possible to move.

He took a long step forward and was at the door. He reached out his hand; his heart knocked at his ribs. Now was the moment of truth: he would twist the knob, push open the door, and.... But his hand was stayed a moment yet by another picture: that of a grinning Sorbma waiting just on the other side of that barrier, waiting to take the door from his grasp the moment he touched the knob. And waiting with him, peering fixedly over his shoulder, the mounted and waxen corpse of Ambrose Bierce.

Oh, God! How could he withstand such a blow?

But it didn't matter what was on the other side of the door—he had to save the Ambroses! He reached for the knob, but his hand never grasped it. The door swung open suddenly, towards him, the knob sharply striking the tips of his fingers. He was half-blinded by the blazing yellow light of the Back Kitchen, but saw that Ambrose Ichabod Sorbma stood before him. And there, peering at him over Sorbma's shoulder—

Sidney reeled away and with a cry flung up his arms, as if to ward off that dread blow. Which fell, and struck him to the floor.

* * * * * * *

"What the Devil!" said a familiar voice. Sidney looked up, past his forearms, to see Bill Ambrose standing in the kitchen door, with Sorbma. "What are you doing?" demanded Bill. Then, with a grin: "Oh, I see. Took you by surprise, did we?"

"He was spying on us," shrilled Coo in delight, peeping over Bill's shoulder. "Caught in the act!"

The Ambroses were not only unharmed, they were in remarkably good spirits. Not so the old fellow with them. He was baffled, confused, lost. He stood with one hand pressed to his forehead, his eyes turning this way and that, as if he were looking about for that triumphant, exultant Sorbma of a few hours ago. He didn't find him...and neither did Sidney, who stared at this defeated ancient with doubtful recognition.

Sidney had fallen over backwards onto the steps and had presence of mind now, barely, to pick himself up. The Ambroses brushed by him contemptuously. Sorbma stood for a moment in the kitchen door, which gaped open as if in dismay, and Sidney saw that the inside of that outwardly-shabby portal was unexpectedly opulent. It was covered with a thick red baize and studded with brass nails—the cloth obviously being meant to stifle sounds—the sounds of screams, no doubt, and which it did...a little. And he saw into the kitchen itself. The blazing yellow light seemed to burn everything into his memory at a glance.

On the wall facing him there were some strange pictures—large reproductions of grisly antique woodcuts depicting torture and cannibalism in newly-discovered lands: naked men hacking apart still-living human beings, with arms and legs hanging on hooks, and severed heads with faces contorted with horror being held aloft by their hair.

Near him, to the left, was a century-old black iron stove on which a pot was boiling and bubbling, and to his right a table crowded with oddly-shaped bottles filled with red and green liquids and powders, like an alchemist's workshop. And lying on the floor before the table were two very large transparent plastic bags, thicker and sturdier than those used for garbage.

After the shadowy dimness of the shop, the blazing light hurt his eyes, and they instinctively sought for relief in a dark aperture at the far left corner of the room. It was a door, slightly ajar, and he could see into the shadowy interior of what was probably once a pantry, and where he now dimly discerned a host of waiting, featureless objects, like discarded clothes-dummies in a department-store basement.

Sorbma saw that he saw and shot him the strangest glance—of astounded, outraged, defeated, hopeless appeal. "Oh, sir!" he wailed, closing the door behind him and falling upon Sidney, as if for support. "Oh, sir, if only *you* were an Ambrose!"

"Here, now!" cried Sidney, struggling to disengage himself.

"They can't take a hint!" croaked Sorbma, clutching desper-

ately at Sidney's lapel. "They have no imagination. Fear," he added in a strangled whisper—and he glanced tremblingly back over his left shoulder, as if to demonstrate what he meant—"fear is everything. Without fear, nothing: the elixir has no potency without despair and horror."

The fearless Bill and Coo led the way out of Sorbma's parlor and into the shop. Behind came Sidney. Behind came Sorbma. Like a parade of conquerors and their dazed captives. The Ambroses, smirking, marched across the shop to the front entrance.

"Now," said Bill, "for this screwy business of the door." He put his finger into the hole where the shaft of the knob had been and pulled. The door came open. *"Voilà!"* Bill looked around, slyly, at Sidney. "You want to know how I knew? Elementary, my dear Fergus. There is no back way out of this place. The damned thing's a fire-trap! And I knew this old fart had to have some way of getting in and out, so...*voilà!*"

Sidney stood looking at the bricks of the alleyway, touched slant-wise by the declining sun. Freedom.

"A deal's a deal, right?" said Coo to the hapless Sorbma, who stared dumbly. "You sell us the shop at the price we agreed on, or we'll spread your name and description over all the local papers and in every collectors' publication and fanzine in the country."

"You'll be famous," promised her husband. "And a fellow like you must be hiding from something."

"It can't be the draft board," said Coo.

"So it must be bill-collectors," said Bill, looking around him with an unspeakable complacency.

"Your aged grandmother in Kokomo," went on Coo, with a fine scorn, "will be able to find you after we're through with you."

"In the dark," added Bill.

"Ohhh, I wouldn't care for that," murmured Sorbma, casting another look back over his shoulder. "She's old, old, old! And I much prefer the company of youth."

The two youths at the door turned a slowly revolving glance around the store, smiling in unanimous proprietary self-satisfaction. Their moving gaze came at last to Sidney and rested on him. The man and wife exchanged an amused glance.

"You look like a fish out of water," said Bill. "Hop in"—with a backward hitch of his head in the direction of the car—"and we'll give you a lift back to civilization."

Sidney, longing for freedom from the shop and still somewhat confused, did as he was bid and followed the Ambroses into the alley, leaving the terrible Mr Sorbma standing in the doorway.

"You know," said Bill, as they walked across the bricks, "that old jerk has a thing about people named Ambrose."

"You should have heard him scream," said Coo, "when we twisted his arm."

Sidney stumbled on the uneven surface. "Twisted his arm...?"

"That's a metaphor, silly! Don't you know anything? I mean when we told him what we were going to do to him if he didn't sell us the shop at a fair price."

Bill chuckled...and Sidney wondered now how he had ever failed to recognize that chuckle, red baize or no; he had heard it often enough. "I don't see why he's so worried about losing the shop. He can always get a job at the Hollywood Wax Museum. But he can keep that collection of figures he has. We don't want *them*." He held open the rear door of the Plymouth. "Won't you step into the back, Mr. Sidney?" Sidney climbed in and deposited himself among the litter of comic magazines. "Where you belong," muttered his host as he slammed the door; "with the trash."

Bill was soon in the driver's seat (where Sorbma had once been long ago, but no more) with Coo beside him, and the car moved down the alley, past the shabby building with the big black letters over its front. The man to whom those letters referred stood in the doorway of the shop which was to be his for such a short time now, looking after them with an expression Sidney couldn't quite decipher: but his self-possession was

evidently returning.

"One thing's for sure," said Bill, "and that is that your friend Jack McMinion is behind all this."

"Jack McMinion!" Sidney stared at Bill's right ear, supposing that his own ears had played him false.

"Of course!" explained Bill, with an almost unutterable scorn for Sidney's obtuseness and a glance of contempt in the rear-view mirror. "Frank Flowers or Micawber's wouldn't try to depress prices like that. They'd just be cutting their own throats. But a pipsqueak like McMinion can pull the temple down upon his own head. He's got nothing to lose."

Sidney continued to stare, but his stare became after some moments more moderate and more comfortable; it softened into a gaze of speculative wonder. It came home to him that the Ambroses were terrible people, in their way. For if he, that horrible old man who clung so desperately to existence by feeding on other people's lives, if *he* were terrible, then they, in being equal to him (at least) were equally terrible. Their moral unimaginativeness made them so. They were untouchable in the innocence of their malice. They were soft and yet heartless. Sorbma had thought to conquer them with his greater power but they had conquered him with their incapacity.... But was that so very surprising? Wasn't it true that in every quarrel between a bright man and a dull man, the dull man always wins? Poor Sorbma! He had had nothing to work with, or to work upon, in dealing with the Ambroses. There was in their breasts no responsive chord which he could strike to awaken that profound despair, that perhaps metaphysical horror, he had sought to inspire in them. Possibly, just possibly, he might have succeeded in intimidating them physically—although his apparent age and feebleness made that unlikely; but he could never have made them feel awe. He had tried, and they had sneered. He head shown them a backward reach of time and a range of evil intention far beyond their small experience...and they had smirked, knowingly. They had looked into the Abyss...and had found it shallow. He, Sidney, had always thought himself to be made

of sterner stuff than they and had felt an amused and rather affectionate condescension toward them on that score. But they, these dumb malicious children in the front seat, had defeated the man who had defeated Ambrose Bierce.

Did he envy them? Did he admire them? Did he want to be like them? No, he decided, turning his gaze out the window to the long street. No, somehow he didn't. Looking into the distant prospect, he seemed to make out, if only sketchily, the outlines of a few things he had barely glimpsed before. This whole question of weakness and strength and their relation to fantasy, romance and imagination was a bit more complicated then he had thought. Perhaps what he had taken for weakness was another kind of strength; or, if not that, one of those graces without which life would be worthless and therefore all strength pointless. Perhaps (ah, perhaps!) Jack had been right and he had too often confused what was stronger with what was better, and not only in his reading.

They stopped a few blocks away at a service station. As they eased out again onto the street, Sidney looked back in the direction of Sorbma's den and saw thick black smoke roiling up into the darkening sky from the spot where he judged the shop to be. He watched it, thinking with a pang of all those first editions, those Finlay and Bok covers; but it wasn't a very sharp pang. It was wistful, rather, for in his mood of the moment such things seemed to him to be part of the vanities of this world.

They drove on. The Ambroses happily congratulated themselves on their *coup* of the day and discussed how they might best meet the bill for Sorbma's shop tomorrow, paying no more attention to their kidnapped passenger in the back than they did to the blaring fire engines which, shuddering redly, shouldered their way past them through the rush-hour traffic.

They released Sidney in front of their store. "Well," said Bill with a malicious grin as he came around from the other side of the car to the sidewalk, "in a few days you'll be able to buy everything you wanted back there. From us. At our prices."

"I think not," said Sidney. "I wouldn't want them in their

present charred condition."

It was their turn to stare. He walked away down the tree-lined street without looking back.

That was some time ago. It has been noted with a conjecturing wonder by the frequenters of the Ambrosia Bookstore that Sidney never comes there anymore. They have also noted that Sidney's book on Ambrose Bierce is still unpublished and they have heard rumors (for people do see him elsewhere) that he seldom mentions the name of that writer these days. They have even heard that he has sold his entire Bierce collection, including some manuscript letters and a very rare photograph, and has given the proceeds to Jack McMinion in payment of some old debt. But they are all agreed that *that* is very unlikely.

THE BOY IN
THE IRON MASK

In the late Summer of 1929, two boys sat on a rustic foot-bridge crossing a wooded stream.

They were talking about *The Man in the Iron Mask*.

"It's showing Saturday at the Strand," said one of the boys, excitedly. "I can hardly wait. There's only one show this time, in the afternoon, because of my Dad's lodge meeting that night. And you can bet I'm not going to miss that show! I've been waiting for it for months. I've read all about it, you know."

He probably had. His name was Philip Carter and he was a great book-worm and movie-goer. Or, anyway, as great a movie-goer as circumstances would allow: the one theatre in his little town opened its doors only on Saturday. In looks...well, the twelve-year-old Phil might have appeared, with his light brown hair and blue eyes, on the cover of *The Saturday Evening Post* as the Representative American Boy—the freckles across the bridge of his nose not yet being obscured by spectacles,

The other boy, who was about the same age, looked as If he had never read a book in his life (perhaps he hadn't, outside of school), but he loved movies almost as much as his friend. "It must be Just about the best motion picture ever made," said this boy, with infinite faith. "You say Douglas Fairbanks plays D'Artagnan? Who's the Man in the Iron Mask?"

"The twin brother of King Louis the Fourteenth," replied the knowing Phil, "and the Rightful Claimant to the Throne."

"King Louis?" said the other boy, "Hah!" For Louis was *his*

name. "I have to see that! But, you know...my mother says a lot of her folks are coming to visit that day and I'll bet she wants me to hang around the house all afternoon."

Phil winced. "Golly, that's a fate worse than death—to miss *The Man in the Iron Mask*. But, look here, if you do miss it, I'll come and tell you all about it. In great detail. Because one thing is certain," he added, settling back rather complacently against the rickety wooden railing that guarded one side of the foot-bridge: which was nothing more than two rows of 2 x 6" slats supported by trestles; "one thing is certain, and that is that I am not going to miss that picture."

There was a noise of squawking protest, not unlike the creaking of a rusty hinge on a barn-door, and the splintery rail against which he was leaning, gave way—tore loose, exposing ugly rust-encrusted nails—and Phil, with a distinct but help-less consciousness of the irony of the situation, found himself sprawling clumsily backward and off the bridge.

He fell towards the water, head downwards but looking up, arms and legs spread. He saw his friend's face framed between his feet: an intensely interested, peering face. Phil's brief life did not pass before his inner eye, but it could easily have done so, for he was able to take note of a good many memories, thoughts and possibilities almost simultaneously. One of the possibilities was that he might drown: for he couldn't swim.

He hit something, something so hard that at first he thought it was one of the round rocks lying at the bottom of the marvel-ously clear stream. But it was only the water itself. It fringed out around him and closed back over him. He sank. He gasped for air and choked on water. It hurt, terribly—like gulping down marbles. He touched bottom and went up again. He struggled and strained for the light and air, his eyes bulging, and saw Lou, far above him, pushing back the nail-barbed railing that had swung back almost into place, and stepping calmly off the bridge, as from the deck of a ship.

He himself had never been so calm, but he knew that no one seeing him would believe that. Eyes and mouth wide, he was

thrashing the water frantically, as if in a paroxysm of impotent rage, like that king in the history books who had ordered the sea flogged because It had balked him. But, inside, he wasn't really upset or afraid at all; and when a hand grabbed him unexpectedly by the hair and he felt himself being tugged backwards to the bank, he resented it as an indignity.

He touched the bank, twisted about, clawed feebly at the grassy slope; lay half in the water, half out, his body shaking as with some inexhaustible grief, water spilling from his eyes, ears, mouth and nose. When the water had ebbed enough so that he could raise his head, he saw Lou's pale face regarding him anxiously. Lou's very pale face—with the strong contrast of a red liquid trickling down the side of his head from his temple and disappearing beneath his wet collar.

"It's nothing," said Lou, with a smile and a grandly casual gesture that Douglas Fairbanks might have envied. "A mere scratch. I hit a rock going down."

Phil scrambled to his feet. "We'd better get up to the house and have Mom take a look at that."

Lou tried to help him up the bank, but needed as much help himself. The two, each thinking he was supporting the other and each being right, trudged the narrow well-scuffed path to Phil's back door, some fifty yards from the creek.

"Now, Lou," exclaimed Phil's mother, as they staggered in, the screen door banging noisily behind them, "Now, Lou, what have you been up to now?" For Lou was the more mischievous of the two and was often in trouble. "My God!" she cried, the next moment, "you're hurt! How pale you are! Come into the living room and lie down on the couch. Lie down, Louie. No, no, never mind—for he had started to protest that he would get the couch all wet...but, despite this scruple, he sank down upon it, anyway. She looked at the "scratch," as he had called it. The very light touch of her agitated fingers caused more blood to gush forth. It matted his hair, spilled upon the cushions, dripped to the rug. "Phil! Run and call Louie's mother while I wash this—no, the doctor first! Run down the road to Dr. Vredenburg's. I'll get the

antiseptic from the cupboard—"

"Don't bother," said the twelve-year-old Louis Julius Ulmann. "Don't bother: I'm dead."

And so it seemed. His eyes glared at the ceiling, the coursing stream of blood slowed to a trickle. Phil's mother stared. A wail burst from her, as if ripped from her, bodily: *"Oh, my God? What shall I tell his mother?—his poor mother!"*

But Lou wasn't quite dead yet. His white lips trembled...and there rose from them into the silence of the room a wraith-like whisper, rather curious and striking.

"Well...*The Man in the Iron Mask* shows Saturday at the Strand, anyway."

* * * * * * *

All this happened on a Thursday. Phil came into the house the next afternoon just as his mother was hanging up the receiver of the telephone on the wall of the hall.

"Phil, the funeral is tomorrow afternoon. Louie's mother wants you to be one of the pall-bearers. You can wear the dark suit we got you for Grandma's funeral: it'll still fit; and I have a pair of white gloves...." She stopped at the sight of his face. "Yes, I know, Dear. He was your best friend, but...."

But there was something in her son's face that made her pause again; something that was not grief.

"I...I want to go to the pictures tomorrow," he blurted. "It's my only chance to see *The Man in the Iron Mask*. They're having that meeting of Dad's lodge in the theatre tomorrow night and they can't show it Sunday because of those darn Sunday laws. If I don't see it tomorrow afternoon, I never will...."

"Listen, Dear, I know you've been looking forward to seeing that show, but this is more important. You'll see many moving pictures in your life, but you won't have many friends like Louie."

His clouded face was lighted by an inspiration. "He would have wanted me to see the picture. His last words were about

The Man in the Iron Mask."

"Oh, Phil! Phil!" His mother shook her head, half-laughing, half-crying. "How can you? Your best friend, the boy who saved your life! Don't you see how it would look if you're not at the funeral? And at a picture show! And it's not only Louie who counts. There's his mother. You're going for her sake, not just for his."

Phil, his fists clenched at his sides, stared, stunned by the threatened loss, at the wreathing pattern of the hall carpet, which looked, he noticed for the first time, something like a large stylized face: a mouth of sorts, a nose of sorts, eyes. His own face was almost as immobile: a mask of sullenness.

His slightly plump, good-natured mother studied him briefly. "Forget about that trashy picture, Phil," she said finally, turning away. "You're going."

She heard a muttered remark escape his clenched teeth— "Oh, I'm going, all right!"—but decided to ignore it.

The next day he made good his word. They were preparing to leave the house for the funeral parlor when Phil broke a long silence to announce that he was going to the bathroom. His lanky father, who was Sheriff of Bunyan County, gave him a cool, appraising glance: for there had been something portentous, almost defiant, in the announcement.

They heard the toilet flush, the water run in the basin. After a while, Sheriff Carter glanced at his watch. "What is he trying to do—see how far he can run up the water bill?" He tried the knob. "Damn! He's locked the door. Phil, Phil!"—pounding; "come out of there."

But there was no response. Carter was almost, but not quite, determined to be mad. His wife, in her dark suit, white gloves and cloche hat, stood looking on. A thought alarmed her. "You don't suppose...?"

That didn't seem very likely to him, really. But his razors were in the cabinet in there and other imaginative boys had tried to kill themselves for reasons just as silly. And from inside the bathroom the sound of the water twisting down the drain

never ceased.

Carter turned and ran through the kitchen and out the back door. As he came around the side of the clapboard house, he saw to his relief that the bathroom window, which swung outward, had been pushed wide open. The step-ladder was lying in the grass some yards away. He propped the ladder against the window, climbed inside the room, turned off the water and, unlocking the door, opened it to reveal his wife's stricken face.

"It's okay, Cora. The kid's run off to that damned show. He won't be there long, though."

Shucking off his dark coat, he made his way, now trotting, now walking, to the picture theatre two streets away. Sometimes his heavy feet fell like hoof-beats upon echoing board sidewalks and sometimes they fell silently enough upon dirt and dry grass; and he was again conscious that Rosewood—a very few years before it had borne the ignominious name of Stumpvllle—might easily lapse back into country, if he weren't vigilant. Chickens scattered from before him. A cow browsing in Mrs. Brown's back yard, a block from the Civic Center, raised her head to look at him as he trotted by. He turned left and therefore West on Main Street, the far end of which (three hundred yards off) was blocked by the Lumber Works, and slowed to a more sedate pace as befitted its metropolitan concrete. Casting a proprietary glance at the combination jail, court-house, post office, and county building across the way, he turned into the entrance of the Strand Theatre. He exchanged a few joshing words with Ed Foley, the manager (and like himself a Dread Potentate of the Masquer's Lodge, meeting this evening) and borrowed a flash-light.

He expected to find Phil sitting about the tenth row back, near the aisle. He didn't, though. To his increasing surprise, he couldn't find Phil at all. He walked slowly, peering up from the front of the theatre in the left-hand aisle. The place was packed for this one showing and not just with kids. All those assembled faces were turned one way, staring at the images floating on the screen: images huge, pale and silent as ghosts. Something in the

64 | ARTHUR JEAN COX

spectacle of so many rapt faces all uniformly addressed in one direction struck him as being both contemptible and chilling. To dispel that slight touch of fear, he turned and glanced at the screen—saw Douglas Fairbanks, in fancy dress, and with his sword drawn, confronting another man with an ugly iron grill or visor strapped to his face. He felt a touch of contempt at the childishness of such play-acting...and then a wry amusement as he thought of the costumes he was going to be seeing in a few hours in this very place. Turning back to his task, he crossed the front of the auditorium to the right-hand aisle. Mrs. Brown, the owner of the cow, thumped the piano.

Sitting in the first seat of the first row on the right-hand aisle was Barney Smith, or Barney Google (as the kids called him), gurgling with a kind of awe-struck happiness as he gazed upwards with his goo-goo-googly eyes (as the kids would say) at the screen. Sheriff Carter laid a heavy index finger on the middle-aged man's shoulder.

"Don't make a fool of yourself, Barney," he advised.

And Barney, abashed, his harmless gaiety extinguished, dropped his eyes to the shadowy floor and fell silent. Carter continued up the aisle, scrutinizing the clusters of childish faces.

There! There was—some kid, not Phil. Puzzled, he peered closely. He knew that face, but couldn't put a name to it, felt that provoking thread of exasperation one always feels in such situations. The boy, about Phil's age, deliberately ignored him for some seconds, then turned a look upon him that was...what? Questioning? Ironic? Insolent? Carter couldn't quite decide. But what did it matter? It wasn't Phil. He moved on. He checked the toilet and even the broom closet, then handed the flashlight back to the politely unquestioning Ed Foley and left, very disgusted with his son and very mystified.

The funeral proceeded well enough without Phil, his place beside the coffin being supplied by a previously-unsuspected cousin. As Sheriff Carter filed by that open-faced crate for the conventional last glimpse, he was surprised by a pang of real pity for the "deceased," as he would have termed him in a

report. Louie lay there so very prim and still—which, of course, wasn't at all like him!—that you might almost have thought that a wax dummy had been substituted at the last moment and the still-living boy was wandering around somewhere, up to his old mischief. He was All Boy, that kid! Not like...well.... And the Sheriff felt another pang, a pang of envy and resentment. Skipping the funeral like this was the only time Phil had shown any real spunk.

They had murmured something to Mrs. Ulmann, Louie's mother, about Phil being sick, and she, poor woman (she was a widow, her husband having been killed some years ago in a logging accident) instantly assumed that he was sick with grief for his friend: a diagnosis that mortified them both considerably. And now, to their further mortification, she insisted on stopping by their place to comfort the sick boy. They humored her, hoping that Phil would be at home and moping in his bedroom when they arrived: that way they could preserve the fiction that he wasn't well.

But he was not at home and it was impossible to pretend that he was. There was some puzzled conjecture among the relatives as to what had happened to him—for, of course, the entire funereal party had come along, and the driveway, yard and road-front of the Carter residence were clogged with their dark cars. There was a general agreement that the boy was wandering about distracted with grief; and one of Lou's uncles, a fat man with a mottled bald head like a creek-bottom stone, went so far as to suggest that the creek be dragged: as if Phil might have gone out to finish what his friend had interrupted. As they speculated, they all ate and drank, and Carter was beginning to remind himself pretty often that he didn't know any of these people other than Mrs. Ulmann. He wanted very much to try on his Masquer's costume and have Cora make any needful alterations before it was too late, but he could hardly do so while they were here. It would be just too ridiculous to appear before the mourners in that yard-wide hat with the white feather, the velvet mask, the black cloak, and the rest of the get-up.

As he was resignedly thinking all this, the bathroom door opened and Phil incongruously issued forth. Everybody stared at him. It wasn't possible that he had been in the bathroom all this time, because several of the visitors had already had, occasion to investigate its interior; and his demeanor, as he raked the assemblage with his eyes, was so obviously defiantly guilty that it was no use pretending that he was either sick or grief-stricken. Mrs. Ulmann, her eyes wide, a half-eaten dish of strawberry ice cream in her lap, raised a trembling and disillusioned hand to her mouth. Phil saw her. His eyes sank and his face reddened— as if reflecting the light of a glowing forge where some iron contrivance was being fashioned (this was his father's audacious simile, remembering how Phil's face had looked standing beside Felix's forge the night they took the quasi-official Buick in for repairs).

Carter brushed by Phil, saying as he did so. "Go to your room," and stepped into the bathroom. Suddenly clairvoyant, he lifted the lid of the clothes hamper and saw lying on the rumpled towels a pair of dime-store glasses, a soft cap and a striped sweater. So! Lon Chaney Junior, huh? The Boy with a Thousand Faces. Or Two, anyway.

After a few minutes, during which he and Cora saw the visitors out (for everyone suddenly became conscious of the time), he followed Phil upstairs and found him sitting forlornly on the side of his cot. They looked at each other for a long moment. Phil was defiant. A low growl escaped him. A very low growl— from the region of his stomach.

"Hungry, huh?" said Carter. "Well, I can understand that. You only had some toast and orange juice for breakfast and I guess you haven't eaten since. Well, young man, you're going to be even hungrier, because you're not getting any dinner tonight. Did you like the picture? We'll talk about it tomorrow morning over breakfast—if I decide to let you have any breakfast."

He stepped back, pulled the door of the room shut and, taking a ring of skeleton-keys from his pocket, locked it; as if it were the door of the solitary (that is, the single) cell of his jail.

"Locked in!"

The prisoner, lying in bed with the sheet pulled up about his bare shoulders, thought of his harsh sentence with some resentment. And he was so hungry too! His stomach stirred restless and muttered faintly, like a sleeper disturbed by a bad dream.

The window to his right, wide open, was like a picture of a summer evening. There were trees nearby (in which he could hear the friendly birds calling to one another); and he could see in the distance, on the other side of the creek, an. upland meadow bristling with fir, spruce and pine, and the peaked roof of a house with a thin thread of white smoke rising straight into the air from its chimney. He lay awake a long time, feeding on his misery, and waiting for the sun to go down—which it did at last, in a blaze of glory, like D'Artagnan fight against overwhelming odds. His room faced West and every detail in it was almost preternaturally visible. The backs of his books on the shelf across the room were gilded with a glowing light. He could easily read the titles: *The Three Musketeers*, *The Count of Monte Cristo*, *The Last of the Mohicans*, *The Jungle Book*, *Alice in Wonderland* (which his father had said only a sissy would want to read), *Peck's Bad Boy* (a gift from his father—not that he didn't like it), a large illustrated Poe, *Jeeves*, and three *Mutt & Jeff* albums. But these things darkened even as he watched, as if the house lights of a theatre were being dimmed....

He was conscious of the room and of everything in it, even of the scene outside his window, but he seemed to be watching, still, *The Man in the Iron Mask*. Douglas Fairbanks, wearing that dread device, towered before him, wavered, and was gone.... Hadn't that been a swell picture? As an impartial critic he was sure of it, but his merely personal enjoyment of it was spoiled for a while when he saw his father walking up the aisle, shining that flashlight into people's faces...saw him stumble, fall forward into the aisle, dropping the flashlight with an astonishing clatter. Startled by the noise, Phil jerked his head back—on his pillow.

He was in bed, his heart beating fearfully. He listened. And heard again the groping, clopping, clattering noise. It was on the stairs...at the top of the stairs...in the hallway, coming towards him. No: It had turned aside...into his mother's room. Of course, it was his father. His father, coming home drunk, had fallen on the stairs. Phil chuckled, picturing the Sheriff drunk in that outlandish costume.

He must have been asleep for some time, he decided, for the moon was visible through the window and it would have taken it some hours to have worked its way so stealthily over his house, lolling his head on the pillow, he saw that a pale oblong of its light had spilt across the floor and was overlapping on one side the toes of some shoes pointing out from the wall next to the door. Which was odd...because his shoes were under his bed. He remembered kicking them—oh. a long time ago!—under the bed as he fretfully plucked off his clothes. So...what were those shoes by the wall? Could they be his father's? No, they were too small. They were a boy's shoes. Could his Mother have bought him a new pair for the funeral and forgot to tell him about them? No...she would never forget something like that.

They were glistening black. The moonlight crinkled on them like cellophane. And how funny those white socks looked. People didn't wear socks like that anymore, going right up to the knee—not boys, anyway, not even with...what were they called? Oh, yes—knickerbockers. Had his father ever worn knicker-bockers? He might have. He was a boy in Chicago back before the Great War. But, really, he wouldn't have worn white stock-ings with them. That would have made him look like a sissy and he wouldn't have stood for that. Black shoes, white socks, blue silk pants...and those white hands hanging out of the white lace cuffs at the side of the pants.

Phil's body stiffened beneath the sheets. He raised his head from his pillow, felt the hairs at the back of his neck prickle.

There was somebody standing beside the door.

He tried to call out—

"Who's there? Who is it?"

—but no recognizable words emerged. An owl mocked him from the creek, but there was no reply from the figure against the wall.

And as he stared, he gradually made out that above the blue silk pants was a white frilly shirt and a jacket, a black velvet jacket, perhaps, because it seemed to drink up the light like a blotter. And above the shirt and jacket there was a face, yes...but this was funny: although the hands were white, the face seemed to be black. Or, anyway, very dark. Could it be Willy Burns, the Negro boy who lived on the other side of the tracks? But how could Willy have gotten into his locked room? Besides, it wasn't exactly a face. It was a face of sorts, but like a face in a cartoon, or....

He was jolted, as by an electric shock. What he was seeing seemed suddenly to have some dreadful meaning.

For he had seen that face before.

This afternoon.

At the Strand Theatre.

It was not a face but a mask. Like the mask worn by The Man in the Iron Mask. But this was a boy.

He called again, louder this time and more intelligibly, but with no more effect than before. The boy in the iron mask neither moved nor spoke, but stood as quietly as....

...As one dead.

And he was in the same room with it, a room with a locked door.

He tried to call out, to call his father who had locked him in with this thing. But each time he raised his voice, it broke under the load of fear, like a weak branch with too much snow on it.

He had to get out. The door was locked but there was another way out of the room. He had hardly had the thought when he found himself stepping out of bed and out the window in his bare feet: for his bedroom window looked out over a slanting surface of roof. Dangerously slipping and sliding on the dew-wet shingles, he scrambled along the roof to the next window and looked in—saw the second floor hallway, carpeted by moonlight, saw

the door of his room, pale and expressionless. He raised the window noiselessly and, stepping inside, padded quickly down the hall, past his door, to his parent's bedroom.

He stood trembling on their dark threshold; partly from the cold, because he wasn't wearing any pajamas or nightshirt. From the right side of the bed there issued a familiar sound: a lumberjack sawing down a tree.

"What is it, Phil?" His mother's voice, from the left: quiet, but fully awake. "Did you climb out through the window?"

"There's someone in my room."

He could feel her eyes studying him in the darkness. But she was out of bed and ready, if necessary, to wake her husband.

"It's a boy," added Phil. "He's wearing an iron mask."

"Oh, my God," sighed his mother, with a weary laugh. "That's what you get for going to bed with an empty stomach."

"It's not a dream, I tell you. He's real."

"Here!" She threw him the cloak his father had worn to his Lodge. "Wrap this around you, my little jaybird, and come down to the kitchen with me. I'll get you a fried-egg sandwich and a glass of milk. And, *shhh*," she whispered conspiratorially, as he wrapped the melodramatic cloak about himself, "don't wake your father."

* * * * * * *

When Phil—who had spent the rest of the night on the sofa in the front room, his head lying on the fringed shawl that hid the ineradicable blood-stains—when Phil and his mother came back from church the next morning, his jailer was still "sleeping it off." So the boy got off lightly most of the day. But there were complications, nevertheless; for when his mother went in to make up his bed, she saw that the small reproduction of Gainsborough's *Blue Boy* next to the door had been defaced. Some childish hand had taken a black crayon and had scrawled over the face, almost obliterating it. She recognized the smudged marks as an attempt to draw a mask. An iron mask,

she supposed.

"Why did you do that, Phil?"

He stared at it. "I didn't. He must have done it."

"*He*?"

Phil, his face guarded, dropped his gaze to the floor.

She repeated her question. An answer escaped him: "The boy in the iron mask. He did it."

She drew back, regarded him anxiously. There was something wrong here. If that was a lie, it wasn't a normal lie. And if it wasn't a lie, if he really believed it....

"Phil," she brought out at last, "you've got to get this iron mask business out of your head."

But he found that harder to do than she to say.

That night he had a short and rather one-sided discussion with his father—for Cora had told the Sheriff about the Boy in the Iron Mask as a kind of wonder. Phil didn't want to sleep in his room, but his father easily induced him to do so and with some show of willingness.

"You don't want me to think you're a sissy, do you?" There could of course be only one answer to that; and it followed—by a series of short logical steps, along which his father conducted him—that he had to sleep in his room that night, had to banish from his mind all such nonsense as Phantom Boys. So he turned, rather early, but after supper—for his mother had insisted on his being fed—he turned, rather early, to the stairs, internally very uneasy but conscious that he was under his father's eye and must put on as brave a show as he could. But he knew that he was never very brave, even at his best. He wasn't like Lou. Lou wasn't afraid. Perhaps, he thought bitterly, perhaps Lou should have been his father's son.

This tine his door was not locked. He put on his pajama bottoms and kept on his socks...in case he should want to leave in a hurry. "Maybe tonight," he told himself, "maybe tonight I won't see him."

He lay awake for some time, repeating that to himself, but he must have fallen asleep at last. Must have: because he woke up.

Woke with a start and lay there wondering what had awakened him. He listened—but heard nothing and saw nothing of which to be afraid; and yet he shivered beneath his single sheet, as if in anticipation of the coming winter. His open window framed a picture of the night sky, sprinkled with stars and decorated with a moon; but his room was very dark. How he hated the dark! If only he dared get out of bed to pull the cord of his light! But he didn't dare and lay trembling in the darkness.

At last, unable to bear the suspense, he quavered, "Are you there?"

There was no spoken answer to this question from the suspended darkness of his room. Or from his dresser. Or from his mirror. Or from his shelf of books. Or from the figure that stood at the far edge of the square patch of moonlight. It was the figure of a boy about his own size and, as he supposed, his own age, and wearing over its face, as on the previous night, an iron visor. It was dressed, again as on the previous night, as if it were on its way to a meeting of the Masquers...although no one so young would have been admitted to that ribald gathering—a thought that was overtaken and shouldered aside by another: What if the Masquers were playing a trick on him? A practical joke? Paying him back for having skipped Lou's funeral? Of course! It was just the kind of thing they would do! He had heard about some of the things those jokers had done, how they had scared Tom Potter so that he stayed sober for months. He grasped at this idea. What was happening was still scary but at least it made sense. It was part of the real world.

But in the next instant he saw something that swept aside this hopeful possibility, something that wrung from him a spasm of sickening disgust and left him prostrate, absolutely convinced of the authenticity of his mysterious visitor. The dark metal beneath the square rectangles of eyes was wet, streaked with tears. The Boy in the Iron Mask was crying,

Phil would have spoken again, but all power of speech and of movement had failed him. He might have said, if he had been able to say anything, that he couldn't possibly become any

more afraid without fainting or dying. But he would have been wrong...as he discovered when that mute figure moved.

It came forward, one hand raised to the grill that concealed its features, the other stretched towards Phil. It advanced slowly, until it stood at the foot of his bed....

And screamed.

No, it was not the Boy who screamed. It was Phil himself. He heard himself screaming—heard, as if he were a long way off.

That was horrible, that was horrible enough, but what was more horrible was that something outside his room was contemptuously dissatisfied with his weak and feeble cry and took it away from him—took it up, enlarged it, deepened it and prolonged it. It was as if his scream had been seconded, voted on and passed unanimously by the Town Council. For the Town screamed. He heard it screaming. Heard the sound of its baritone howl overflow the town and spill across the countryside. Heard Bombazine, the neighbor's black Scotch terrier, bark in terror. Heard all the dogs of the town bark, the dogs across the creek, in the upland meadow and over the hill; heard their small frenzied yaps, yelps and howls puncturing and dotting the long wavering surface of that scream...which stunned all thought and made the hair on his head crawl and bristle, which rattled the mirror above his dresser, rattled the picture of the *Blue Boy* on the wall, rattled the glass of his window. And from the corner of his eye he glimpsed through the window a flutter of white, a figure all in white, like a conventional ghost, or like a man in his nightshirt, running along the path on the other side of the creek.

The sight of that running thing, the example it showed, the proof that movement was possible, freed him from his paralysis. Still screaming, he flung the bedclothes up and forward with all his might and in the same movement sprang out of bed. His sheet fell over the speechless thing that stood at the foot of his bed, as if to snuff it out, and Phil, looking back as he wrenched open the door of his room, saw it standing there draped with the sheet like an unveiled statue. He ran—ran forward, through the scream as through a resisting medium and through a haze of

light, ran buffeting from side to side down the narrow hallway. And collided with something—with something, with someone, as substantial as the thing in his room, which caught him and whirled him aloft in powerful arms and shook him,

"Phil! Phil! For God's sake, control yourself!"

The scream that had so filled the house and the town and the night ended with a dying fall, a wail trailing away...and Phil heard only his own pitiably small and lonely voice...which likewise lapsed and trailed away. And the silence that followed seemed for a moment as thick as cotton wadding: as if he had been deafened by that scream and would never hear again.

But his father noisily moved. He shoved Phil into the bedroom and his mother's arms, turned, ran down the hall, his shirt fluttering, a boot under one arm. They heard him clattering down the stairs, heard the front door slam.

"Honey," said Phil's mother, "it's all right. You're in no danger. It's probably just a fire at the Mill."

"It's not that. He's in my room again. The Boy in the Iron Mask."

"You've been dreaming, Dear. The siren woke you from a nightmare."

"No, no, he's real. I saw him."

"All right, Dear; all right," humoring him. "You can stay here till your father gets home."

His father was home in an hour.

"Jesus Christ!" he groaned. "It was that Barney Google. He got into the Mill looking for a place to sleep and somehow—by accident, maybe, or mischievously, or insanely, who knows?—he pulled the cord of the siren and hung on. Woke up the whole damned town! There must be fifty people out in the street! We found him hiding behind a stack of lumber, whimpering and trembling like a whipped dog. Something has to be done about that nut. The Town Council is meeting Wednesday and they're going to give Barney his walking papers. *I'll* see to that. Rosewood can do without a town lunatic. He's going to be on that train Wednesday night."

"But, Dear, where will he go? He's lived here all his life."

"That's too long. He should have been gotten rid of years ago." Wrenching off his right boot, he froze, stared. "What are you doing here, Phil?"

"I told him he could sleep here tonight," said Mrs. Carter.

"Good Lord, are you such a sissy that a siren scares hell out of you?"

"It's not that. He saw the ghost again."

Carter held his position, his expression that of a man realizing that he's going to be sick at his stomach. He got up off the bed, lurched towards Phil, his half-removed right boot dragging horribly. "You're making that up!"

"No, I'm not. He's real. I saw him."

"I won't have that, Phil," said Carter quietly. He slapped Phil very hard on the right side of his face and, bringing his hand back, hit him back-handed on the other side.

The boy reeled back, eyes wide with shock.

"Henry!" cried Mrs. Carter. "What's got into you? What are you doing—?"

"I won't have that," repeated the Sheriff. "If you've been telling a story, okay—I'll overlook it this time. But I won't have you seeing things. I won't have you like Barney—"

Phil cried—or, rather, yelled—"He's real, I tell you! He was in my room,"

Carter raised his hand again, but his wife, who had come around from the other side of the bed, caught his arm. "What do you think you're doing?—interrogating a prisoner?" Her husband looked at her with something of Phil's look: as if she had struck him across the face.

"Go back to your room, Phil," said his mother, with unaccustomed authority. "The hall light is on and you can keep your light on and the door open."

Sheriff Carter said nothing, but he eyed his son as the boy got up and left the room. And Phil, glancing back, thought that he would never forget that look as long as he lived. He knew that in his father's eyes he was a coward...and perhaps something less

blamable but worse.

Lying again between the rumpled sheets in his glaring room, his Visitor harshly dispelled, he heard his parents arguing in low voices far into the night. His last thought as he drifted off to sleep, and his first when he woke, was: *My dad thinks the wrong boy died in that accident.*

* * * * * * *

Doctor Vredenburg, who kept a combination hospital and sanitarium not a hundred yards down the road, dropped in just after supper the following day. The first intimation Phil had that the man was coming was when he heard the familiar pleasant chuckle of the doctor's Model A Ford fall silent in front of the house instead of musing its throaty way on past.

Rotund and grey, with the cheerful thoughtful face of a country priest, this man was the licensed Free Thinker of the town: tremendously radical in his opinions, but so very necessary—there was only one other doctor in the county—that people smiled rather than frowned at his eccentricities. He boasted Baltimore as his birthplace, but though exiled (for his opinions, it was thought) to these Pacific backwoods, he kept his finger on the pulse of the times. He had subscriptions to *The American Mercury* and *The Dial*, and it was said that he had known Mencken, George Jean Nathan and Sinclair Lewis personally: men whose massive, if rather cloudy, visages he would have carved, if he had had his way, upon Mount Shasta.

Phil's father and mother excused themselves, pleading kitchen duties, and the boy found himself alone in the living room with this awesome personage. He felt a premonitory chill. Could it be that the Doctor had come to see him?

He had. The physical examination was routine and brief. Phil had no fever and his reflexes were normal. But the questions that followed were far more searching than any that had ever been put to him, questions about The Boy in the Iron Mask and questions that had nothing to do with Him but were personal,

horribly personal. This man, so much softer than his father, was far more ruthless in his way. He seemed to want to, and to be able to, lean forward and poke his chubby fingers into every secret place. Phil, standing directly before him, was unable to look away from the Doctor's face and yet he could hardly be said to see it.... It floated before him in a kind of haze. Paralyzed and helpless, he wanted to shrink out of sight, to get away from this terrible man and his terrible questions—questions that went on and on and on until, finally, almost choked by fear, mortification and smothered indignation, he cried out:

"He's real. God damn you! He's real! That's all there is to it!"

And he buried his face in his hands, his fingers covering his eyes...but when he raised them from that grating, they were dry and hard. The Doctor watched his face, his eyes moving slightly back and forth as if he were reading something written there... and he seemed to draw some conclusion from what he saw. There was something of commiseration in his face as he settled back in his easy chair, but something also of satisfaction, as he reached for his pipe. "That's okay, Phil. Ask your father and mother to step in here, will you?"

When Mr. and Mrs. Carter came back into the room, Phil was sent upstairs to bed. He mounted the steps slowly, his legs trembling and weak from his ordeal. The Doctor's disembodied voice floated up to him. "Forgive me.... This is an embarrassing question to ask, but...has there been any, ah, eccentricity or mental trouble in either of your families?"

"Not in mine! You can bet on *that*." And Phil, looking down over the banister, felt for perhaps the first time in his life, a twinge of contempt for his father. He went on to his room, his dreaded room, leaving the door open. His mother's voice was slower in reaching him, and when it did he couldn't make out the words.

"Sure there was, Cora!" His father's voice was emphatic. "You remember that uncle of yours you've told me about. The minister who used to go out in the woods and preach to himself and beat his Bible to pieces."

"Well," the free-thinking Doctor's voice was very dry, "It's hard to tell with religious people."

"Why, no, Henry!"—the voice of Mrs. Carter rose into hearing: "He was my uncle by marriage. His wife, Aunt Leona, was my blood-relative."

There was a throaty chuckle, as if the Doctor were doing an impersonation of his car. "That's good. Insanity isn't transmittable by marriage. Except to the children, of course. Why... thank you. Sheriff! My throat *is* a trifle dusty. I'm not in any danger of being arrested if I drink this, am I?" The Model A idled again in the living room; and Phil knew that his father had brought out from behind the Encyclopedia the glasses and bottle of whiskey appropriated from a bootlegger. He turned on his light and stood looking about his room, involuntarily twitching when he surprised a startled and apprehensive face in the mirror above his dresser.

As he undressed, he heard his name mentioned again downstairs. "You're both grown-up people and I won't disguise from you that his hallucinating like that—for, believe me, he thinks he did see that boy—is alarming. Very alarming. That mustn't be blinked. But you both tell me there's no history of insanity in your families and that gives us grounds for hope. It means that there's no constitutional psychic weakness in Phil, so all this nay be nothing more than a passing crisis brought on by extreme guilt-feelings at having skipped the funeral of the friend who saved his life to go to that moving picture show. Forgive me, but it's almost beautiful! It's a classic case of a Guilt Complex. That boy who comes to see him is, of course, the embodiment of his guilt. We can guess whose face is under that mask, can't we? And, of course, if he could be brought to admit he did wrong, his friend's visits would cease."

Sheriff Carter's voice dropped an octave. "If that's what it takes, then that's what he's going to do." Phil, sliding between his sheets, allowed himself a sad and bitter smile.

"No, no, don't bully the boy. If he simply parrots the right words because you're holding a gun to his head, it won't do any

good. He has to admit it to himself, not to you. You should never use force on unstable persons—and Phil *is* rather unstable. Just now, anyway. If he becomes any more so, if he continues to see this Boy in the Iron Mask, perhaps he should come and stay with me for a while at the sanitarium, where.... No, no, Cora, don't upset yourself. It's just a thought. We haven't come to that yet. Well, that's really all I have to say about Phil at the moment... but, Sheriff, there is another matter I'd like to discuss with you. I hear a rumor that you're planning to run Barney out of town."

"That's something I was going to take up Wednesday at the town meeting, Doc. I would have told you and the others about it then. I know all you old timers knew Barney's family, but they're all dead now and there's no reason for him to hang around Rosewood. Here he's a public eye-sore, but in San Francisco, for instance, he wouldn't bother anyone much; he'd be lost in the crowd of other drifters...."

"That's exactly why he shouldn't go there! Here we all know him and can look after him. Look: I got him a job today, and if he needs a place to sleep I can easily supply him with one...."

"Nothing doing, Doc. I know you're being kind, but a lumbering town like Rosewood can't afford to keep around someone with that taint in his blood. What if he starts playing with matches?"

"Sheriff, when it comes to matches, Barney has as much common sense as you have."

"Sorry, Doctor. I'm putting the matter before the village fathers Wednesday and. if I know them, they'll go along with me."

"Well, here's one member of the Council who'll vote against you! You're sitting on my coat, Sheriff. Coffee? No, thank you, Cora. I have to drive to Arcady to see a patient, and coffee intoxicates me." There was the sound of the front door being unlatched. "It's cooled off a bit, hasn't it?" observed Vredenburg, his voice again very dry.

Phil, lying beneath a patchwork quilt (for the doctor's weather-diagnosis had been correct) heard his mother coming

slowly up the stairs and into his room. "Dear, the Doctor says you're going to be all right."

"I heard what he said, Mother. He thinks I'm crazy...but I'm not."

"No, no, my dear boy. I know that. I'll tell you what. School doesn't start for another month. Why don't you and I go away for a few weeks to the City"—she meant San Francisco. "There's a talking picture playing there, *Broadway Melody of 1929*. Wouldn't you like...?"

"Yes, yes, Mother. Don't cry. We'll go away, if you like. But not tomorrow. I have a couple of things to do first."

The doorway was darkened by his father's gaunt form. "Phil...if you like, we can make up a bed for you on the floor of our room."

"Thanks, Dad. But, you know, I think I might as well sleep in here." His voice was calm, "mature"—as if he were the sane age as the Sheriff...who was a little surprised by his tone.

"Okay, Phil. You can keep your light on and the door open and we'll keep ours open. Come to bed, Cora."

His mother, after several parting caresses, went out of the room,

Phil propped his pillows behind him against the wall and sat up in bed, his hands folded before him on the colorful blanket. He sat there a long time. Then, getting stealthily out of bed, he moved to the door of his room and stood listening. The house was silent. His father and mother were in bed and probably asleep. He tiptoed out into the hall and pulled the string of the hall-light: neither the click nor the expunging darkness evoked any sound of surprise from his parents' room. He stepped back into his own room and very quietly closed the door. He pulled the string of the naked bulb hanging from the ceiling and the room plunged into night, like a stone dropped down a deep well—plunged into a night at first absolute and somehow grateful. He moved back to his bed, bumping his shins, and groped his way between his sheets. His eyes slowly adjusting to the darkness, he carefully rearranged his pillows and sat up in

bed, with his back to the wall.

And waited.

The silence deepened hour by hour and still he sat patiently waiting, his hands folded on the coverlet before him, his calm face addressed to the expectant darkness. Any onlooker would have said that he had never seen a boy so calm, a boy so unlike that boy who had pummeled the water in imitation of the Persian king.

He had no clock but his heart. The long hours pulsed away, until the lower rim of the moon warily showed itself at the upper edge of his window...and still he sat, patiently waiting.

And heard a sound, a liquid sound, so faint that he thought at first it was but the memory of his mother weeping. But, no; It was touching, if very lightly, his outer ear: a single cobweb-strand of sound, barely tangible but real. It was so faint that it might have been the sound of the creek some fifty yards away... if the creek ever made a sound, which it never did. The moon-light crept across the floor and he gradually made out that the weeping came from a figure sitting in his solitary chair on the other side of the door. The figure's face was lowered into its hands. Its shoulders shook slightly, but there was no other move-ment. It was weeping quietly, as if in exhaustion and despair.

Phil stepped out of bed, stood for a moment contemplating that huddled shape. Then, slowly, he approached it.

"Can I help you? Please—is there anything I can do?" The sound of the weeping ceased. Phil, moving one cautious foot at a time, paced closer, like a schoolboy walking across a grave-yard at midnight on a dare. And yet he was absolutely unafraid. The shoulders behind the heavy bowed head ceased their slight quivering. The Boy in the Iron Mask was listening...listening to hear again those words.

"Can I help you?" repeated Phil, taking another step forward. The figure raised its face from its hands and revolved its mask, like a turret, towards him. Phil repeated his supplicating ques-tion...and the Boy raised trembling fingers to the visor that imprisoned its features and the clasps that encircled its head.

"Yes. Yes. I know. You want the mask removed. I'll help you to get it off. I don't know how...but I'll try."

He reached out and touched the mask. It was cold, hard, coarse-grained and dull to the touch. It reflected no light, except below the eyes where it was streaked with tears. It was substantial. As was also the pale hand that rose and clutched him by the wrist: clutched it so firmly that for a moment he felt it would be as difficult to remove as those iron bands. But he was proof even against the panic that that clasp, the clasp of desperate gratitude, might have induced: the iron had entered into his soul. And he pressed on:

"Come into the back yard. There are tools there." The Boy in the Iron Mask rose and the two boys went out of the room, down the hallway and down the stairs, side by side. They might have been twins—the Corsican Brothers, say; for they were very similar in build. They went out the back way of the house. Phil closing the screen door noiselessly behind them. The moon was very bright, touching every familiar object with a sidelong light. Bombazine, the black Scotch terrier from next door, was standing beside the woodpile. He raised his head with its pointed ears and gazed, eyes wide and voiceless, at the two figures crossing the yard. But, surely, he had seen two boys before? What was there here to strike him motionless and dumb? The trees beyond the fence waved their branches slowly, as if in a state of calm madness.

At the far end of the yard was a shed which served as a garage for the stately, officious Buick. The shadow of an owl glided across its tin roof. The two figures—no on-looker could have said which was the more spectral; but there was no on-looker, save the dog, who stood, still staring—the two figures were swallowed up in the gaping blackness of the shed. Bombazine listened. Uncertain, groping noises came from within the dark interior; and then the sound of metal beating on metal.

Clink! clank! clink! Bombazine shuddered, turned and fled.

Clink! clank! clink! The anvil chorus went on, monotonously, bar after bar. One might have thought the house would be

alarmed. And so it was. A light flashed on in the second story—in the bedroom of Phil's parents. It was joined by another, that of the hallway, and by a third on the west side of the house: in Phil's nighted bedroom. A name was called. There was no answer but the sound of metal on metal. *Clink! Clank! Clink!*

Phil's father showed at the back door of the house. He peered out, girding his robe thoughtfully about him. The screen door banged. He strode across the yard towards the shed. Phil's mother stared down from above, framed by the lighted window of her bedroom. She saw her husband vanish into the darkness of the shed.

The beating of metal on metal broke off. Silence. She anxiously stared and waited. And then, amazed, heard the banging start again: metal on metal, the same tempo, the very same touch, as before.

Abruptly another metallic note was struck: a single note, discordant, peremptory, final. It was followed by a cry that startled and froze her, that caused her hand to leap to her throat and flutter there—such a cry as must have greeted the fall of the Bastille, such a shriek as might have escaped the throat of a prisoner when the door of his cell is thrown open: a cry elated and free and yet, like that prisoner, bearing the marks of long despair. It was followed by...nothing; a silence at last gratefully broken by the magnified creaking of an unseen door. And she saw a boyish figure appear on the far side of the shed. It walked away down the dirt lane bordered by the field whose lower edge was soaking and crumbling in the fatal creek. Could it be Phil? Where was he going in those white socks?

The figure, as if in response to these questions—although she had not broken the silence with any profane call—turned its face towards her: a face she saw distantly as a chiaroscuro of moonlight and shadow. She stared, desperately. It was as difficult, and as easy, as trying to see a face in an ink blot. Could it be—? It looked like—but, no, it couldn't be *that* face from so long in the past (for the best and most homelike of women has her secrets). No, that was an illusion of moonlight and distance.

Was it really Phil, then? The figure went on down the dark lane, the white socks twinkling, fluttering, from sight.

Below her, two other figures emerged from the shed into the yard. A boy and a man. The man's right arm was draped in a comradely way about the boy's shoulders; suspended from his hanging left arm was something which the night gave her an excuse for not recognizing. The man was her husband. The boy—she stared again; sighed, with a quick unobserved smile—the boy was her son. But of course it was her son. Who else could it possibly be but Phil?

She hurried downstairs to meet them, doing so at the foot of the stairs abutting on the front room. Her laconic husband raised and gestured with the thing he held in his hand—and tossed it into the front room where it fell heavily upon the sofa, upon the fringed shawl that hid the bloodstains,

Mrs. Carter glided forward, strained towards it: and it, grim as some old instrument of torture, gazed back up at her.

* * * * * * *

Later that morning, Doctor Vredenburg's car again lapsed into silence in front of the house. The Sheriff had come back from his office briefly to meet the Doctor, so the entire Carter family was present in the living room. Unclouded sunlight, warm and sane, poured in through the curtained windows.

"I understand," said Vredenburg, with a glance at Phil, "that there are new developments?"

"That's right," said Carter. "I saw him myself last night. The Boy in the Iron Mask."

Vredenburg gave him a look that conveyed instantaneously and involuntarily the unspoken thought: "So, the insanity *is* on your side of the family, after all?"

"No, no!" said the Sheriff, replying, with a touch of asperity to the look. "Here's the evidence. See?"—removing the mask from behind a sofa cushion. "He's as real as you and I are. And, furthermore, I know who he is. Generally, anyway. I don't know

his name, but he's a second cousin or perhaps a nephew of mine. You see, I have some second cousins in Missouri who have always been...well, rather funny. Eccentric in their behavior. When we were talking last night, I didn't mention them because they're too distantly related to me to be worth mentioning. Second cousins. It sounds odd, but they all have a peculiar look, they all resemble each other, and I can usually spot one of them on sight, even if I've never net him before. Well, this kid is one of them."

Phil favored his father with a long and curious look (as did his mother, though more discreetly). For he too had recognized the boy. When he had struck that last decisive blow with the hammer, the sound it made startled him terribly; and there rang through him, like an echo of that sound, a thought, wild but unutterably compelling: *If the face is Lou's—if this is somehow Lou—I'll go away and leave him here to be a son to my father.*

But when the heavy mask had dropped to the floor, a single shaft of moonlight piercing down through a hole in the tin roof of the shed had fallen upon the ecstatically upraised face of the Boy, and Phil saw, with an unspeakable relief and gratitude, that the face was his own.

"I was so surprised," went on his father, "especially by that cry of joy he let out when Phil got the mask off—Phil insisted on doing it himself—that before I could say two words (and me the Sheriff!) he'd turned and walked out the back door of the shed and was gone. What in the world the kid thought he'd been doing. I don't know for sure. We never lock our doors—don't have to, in this part of the country—and he might have been sneaking into the house every night just to scare Phil here; although he certainly didn't last night, did he, Phil? Or maybe he wanted help in getting the mask off. That's more likely. He certainly couldn't have put that mask on, himself, so some grown-up has been mistreating him. And it was put on since last Saturday, I know that. For this is what's strange, too: I saw him Saturday at the Picture theatre when I went to look for Phil, only I didn't recognize him at the time. Jimmy"—James Boyle

was Sheriff Carter's sole deputy—"is out looking for him now and if he's still in this neck of the woods, we'll pick him up."

Vredenburg had dropped into an easy chair. He now got up, like a man rising to address a meeting. A Town Council meeting, say. He cleared his throat. "Great, Sheriff, great! I'm glad everything turned out so...so unexpectedly well." He moved towards the door, paused, looked back, evidently checked by a thought: a casual thought, of no great importance. "By the way, Sheriff, I hope you've had time to think over our other little discussion of last night. You know, the one about Barney. I'd hate to see him run out of the county, despite that—what did you call it?—that 'taint in his blood'."

The Sheriff studied the phlegmatic doctor closely...as if it were slowly dawning on him that he had seen that face before. On a Wanted poster, perhaps. Then: "Okay, Doc. If you've gotten him a job, like you say, and if you'll keep an eye on him, it'll be okay with me if he stays on." Phil felt an inward amusement that wouldn't have been out of place in someone twice his age. Mrs. Carter turned away to straighten an antimacassar.

"The patient will live," said Vredenburg, looking around with an air of satisfaction. "So long. I have a couple of calls to make."

"That old fart!" snorted Carter, the moment the door had closed behind the doctor. "Him and his 'classic guilt complex': So that boy was 'the embodiment of guilt,' was he? He was the embodiment of flesh and blood!"

Phil thought his father was right. And the doctor too. He thought that the Boy was real, in that he was tangible, in that he came from the outside, but that he also had something to do with, what came from the inside: with dreams, wishes, memories and guilt. He saw, or thought he saw, that the usual ideas about ghosts, spirits, demons, what have you, were simply too limited: they didn't cover all cases. But he didn't bother to mention what he thought. He knew that neither the shrewd and experienced Sheriff or the sagacious Doctor would be much interested in the speculations of a twelve-year-old boy on such a subject.

The Sheriff now asked, "Where are you going, Phil?"

"Oh…just out. I have a couple of calls to make too." And his father and mother smiled at the solemnity of this announcement.

His first call was on Lou's mother.

"Lou saved me from drowning. He saved my life. And I wouldn't even go to his funeral. I went to the moving pictures, instead—"

He hadn't meant to cry, but found he couldn't go on. The water rose and choked him. It was almost as if he were drowning again. He bowed his head in her ample lap, gasping for breath, like a shipwrecked sailor washed ashore.

"Listen to me, Phil," she said, stroking his hair, gently. "Listen. I wouldn't tell anyone but you this. But Louie came to me last night. I saw him just as plain as I see you now. He was dressed like he was going to some sort of fancy party—I think maybe he was. He was sad, but he was happy too. And he asked me to forgive you. And I do."

Phil had one more visit to make. For he believed in keeping his promises.

Barney Smith, otherwise Google, proudly discharging his new duties (that is, poking about with a hoe among the weedy graves and tombs of the cemetery where he was now employed as a caretaker) paused and looked on, unobserved, for some minutes at a young boy who was standing by that new grave. The kid was just standing there, looking down at the freshly turned earth, and—Barney felt a thrill of sympathetic identification—talking to himself. Funny thing: he was telling out loud the plot of that motion picture that had shown Saturday at the Strand. In great detail.

"And, Lou," he heard the boy conclude: "Lou, it was such a *swell* picture!"

THE SLAVES OF MOXON
AND OTHER TALES OF
SCIENTIFIC ROMANCE

Edited and with an Introduction by Philip Newbegin

INTRODUCTION

Here is a fascinating field of writing never before explored, an odd little corner of our national life that has passed almost unnoticed. I say *almost*, for I suppose that at one time or another everyone has glimpsed among the hundreds of pulps on sale at the magazine racks of train stations, drug stores and corner news-stands certain publications with garish covers depicting rocket ships and fantastic tentacled creatures. These are the Scientific Romance pulps, and the book you hold in your hand is a selection of stories from them. It is, of course, unique, the only collection of such writings ever assembled; the first and possibly the last of its kind. Yes, I know.... You smile. You have a shrewd idea as to what to expect from such half-penny a word writing. But read, if you please, any three or four of the twenty-two stories gathered here. Read *The Slaves of Moxon*, say, or "The Venus from Mars," or "Recalled to Life," or "Edison's Greatest Invention." Read them if only to satisfy your detached and intelligent curiosity. Perhaps you will find that you have awakened a thirst or hunger that cannot be satisfied by this one volume, fat as it is. You smile again...but you can't say I didn't warn you.

I speak from personal experience. One dark winter evening, as I waited on the platform of the Philadelphia station for the 5:22, my eye was caught by the exceptionally lurid cover of a magazine and I decided to buy it. It had occurred to me that I might write an amusing little feature on this type of publication for *The Cleona Call-Bulletin*, a small town newspaper for which I have the honor to be reporter, assistant editor, copy-writer, proof-reader, janitor and what have you. I read the magazine (the February 2010 issue of *Edison's SCIENTIFIC ROMANCES*) on the train all the way to Cleona...and far past it, too: for, wrapt in a story, I missed my town. I had to take a train back, from a country station and didn't arrive home until well past curfew (which of course is still observed in Cleona). I felt like a guilty wretch, sneaking through the back streets to my house, the loud and glaring pulp muffled under my coat. Above all else, I dreaded meeting our local constable, but more because I feared Tom's boisterous humor than his officious wrath.

This was a significant incident, although I didn't quite realize it at the time. I visited my local drugstore the next morning before breakfast and bought two similar publications; and, as if that weren't enough, I dropped into Bob's Tobackazine before dinner to scout out a dozen old issues of *Edison's*. Research material, you see. I read them far into the night and about one A.M. began to have some thoughts that surely would have pained my employer, the excellent publisher and editor George Holzapfel, if he had known of them; for I began to suspect that I might be able to place my article with one of the large New York City newspapers (one of the eight would surely take it) or possibly with *Scribner's Monthly*. But, even as I had the thought, I knew that if no one published what I wrote on the subject I would go on reading the magazines, anyway, for my own unprofitable entertainment. I had become an addict.

It was to *Scribner's* that I finally sent my essay, but not before I had thrown a sop to my conscience by giving George a shorter piece for the *Call-Bulletin*. To my surprise, *Scribner's* actually

bill-boarded my title on the cover (though not my name, which would have meant nothing to readers of a national magazine) and, to my further surprise, the piece called forth a spate of letters from all over the country. It seems that there are, out there, many persons who have been slyly reading "that Edison stuff" for years and now were delighted to discover that there were others like themselves—in fact, some writers were unmistakably relieved to discover that others shared their shameful vice. But these surprises were by no means the first I had received. That came when I visited the Philadelphia Yahoos.

I had gotten the name and address of the Yahoos from a squib in *The Rocket* and, noting that it was but two blocks from the Morgan Free Library to which I had to return some books, I decided to pay them a visit. The surprise occurred when I walked into the clubroom—the Yahoos meet every Thursday evening at the back of a bicycle shop—expecting to see a room full of boys and found myself instead in the midst of a gathering of adults, several with heads considerably greyer than mine. This was very early on, you understand, just three days after I had bought my first copy of *Edison's* and two days after I had picked up *The Rocket*, and, until then, the piece I had planned to do was to be a humorous bit on the reading habits of boys. But now I had to change my tune a little; especially when I found that the adults into the midst of whom I had so patronizingly blundered (one eyebrow slightly raised, a faint smile playing about my lips) were not, as you might think, unlettered mail-carriers and bicycle repairmen and such like. Not entirely, anyway. There *was* a mail-carrier there (well-lettered) *and* a bicycle repairman (the owner of the shop), but there was also a lawyer, a professor of astronomy, an engineer, a librarian, a medical man, two writers of scientific romances and the editor of one of the magazines. All seemed to be proud of reading "S-R," as they familiarly called it, although mixed in with their pride was a most curious little touch of defiance. They were not only proud of reading it, of knowing a tremendous lot about it, of having absolutely staggering collections of the magazines,

but also of their own publications, of which more in a moment. But, first, I should explain just what the Yahoos are.

Their self-deprecatory name is taken of course from Swift's *Gulliver's Travels* and was suggested to them by Mr. Lewis Denholm, the editor-owner of the magazine, *Gulliver*. He is the founder and president-emeritus of the club, or "cog-mesh," as some would have it. All intense *devoteés* of science-romance (or "S-R," as they term it) call themselves "cogs," a word some say is derived from *cognoscenti* and others from a pep-talk once given by Edison to a conclave of his readers to the effect that they were all "cogs in a great machine." I prefer the first deriva-tion myself. The Boston *Cognoscenti*, a group closely associated with *The Rocket*, insist that they, and they only, have the right to be called "cogs"; all others are "buffas," Edisonians, "eddies," or mere readers. They base this claim on their oft-repeated belief that they were first on the scene; but this is disputed by the Yahoos, the Peoria Galactics, and the Sons of Edison—this last being a nation-wide pen-pal club that sprang up more or less spontaneously from the letter columns of *Edison's SCIENTIFIC ROMANCES* in the late '20s and '30s and so would seem to have (*pace*, Yahoos!) the strongest claim to priority.

Many cogs publish magazines of their own. There is, in fact, an astonishing number of these—amateur magazines cheaply printed or even more cheaply stenciled, flooding forth from cellars, basements,, backyards and club-houses all across America. They are called "lilipubs," a contraction of "Liliputian publications," as they are mostly small in size and in circulation and because the first ones were published under the protective wing of the ever-enterprising editor of *Gulliver*. A few discuss the literary merits of stories or their scientific bases, one (*Cog/nizance*) purveys news of the field, but most seem to be grab-bags of haphazard commentary, leaning rather heavily on letters, the minutes of club meetings, amateur fiction and artwork and upon any and every kind of discussion and polemic. Some of these are of great personal charm—my favorite is Peter Dunne's

Laputa[1]—but many are given over entirely too much to scientific and philosophical controversy of an unmistakably Laputan flavor.

There is something I should mention in connection with these controversies. I have heard it said that most readers of science-romance are Free Thinkers. This is far from being true. Most are at least nominally church-goers and there are several ministers prominent in the clubs, one of whom, the Reverend J. Holbrook Vance, has become a popular writer in the field. I should add, too, that, despite the unfortunate incident with Frank Fergusson and despite another even more disturbing matter—the conviction of E. Everett Boorman, founder of *The Boy Experimenter* (now combined with *The Rocket*), for an offense which decency forbids me to specify—it would be difficult to find a more innocent group of people than those who band together as cogs. There are no hard drinkers among them, none that I know of, and not many smokers. Can you imagine spending an evening in a gathering made .up almost entirely of men[2] and not hearing a single ribald joke or a single word of profanity? To experience this rare phenomenon, all you need do is attend a meeting of the Philadelphia Yahoos, or, I dare say, any other mesh of cogs.

Looking back over what I've just written, I see I may have

---

1. This is the name, as you will remember, of the flying island inhabited by abstract-minded savants in Gulliver's Travels—a good title, although the unhappy Frank Fergusson had cause to regret it. His luggage was searched by customs officials when he visited Cuba in 1983 and they found two copies of the odd-looking publication in his carpet-bag. As he didn't speak Spanish, he had no idea that the title of the magazine (printed in evenly spaced square-block letters) was an unprintable word, or phrase, in that language and he spent two months in prison under rather distressing conditions before his family managed to ransom him. His account of his arrest and incarceration circulated in his lilipub, Erewhon, makes harrowing reading.

2. Women, so alive to the romance of everything else, are not much taken with the romance of science. Of course, there are notable exceptions, one of whom (as you will discover on perusing the biographical paragraphs with which I have prefaced each story) seems to me very notable indeed.

given a false impression: that when I walked into the clubroom of the Yahoos that first evening I was like a boll-weevil in the middle of a cotton patch. That was hardly the case. Most of the heads there were no greyer than mine and there actually were two boys present, young men no older than fifteen or sixteen but wise beyond their years in the ways of science-romance. However, one person there was so old that the word "elderly" no longer did him justice, and he alone (well...with just a wee bit of help from Lewis Denholm) accounts for the impression I have of hoary antiquity whenever I think of that fateful visit. This was Mr. Thibault de Castries...or Dr. de Castries, as he styles himself, although the provenance of his doctorate is obscure. He seemed to be the most distinguished person present; such, anyway, was my impression at the time. He eclipsed not only the astronomy professor but even the editor (but only, perhaps, because Mr. Denholm is such an *habitué* of the place). He didn't to my mind quite eclipse Dr. Karl Fredericks, who had served for four years as medical officer aboard the trans-Atlantic zeppelin, *The Silver Cloud*, and who had some fascinating anecdotes to tell; and he certainly did not eclipse, or cast the slightest shadow upon, H.-J. Augenblick...but I won't attempt any description now of these two writers, as each has a story included here, with an appended biographical paragraph.

To get back to Mr. de Castries: he was the person most looked up to that evening...or down to, I should say, as he is, in his mere physical aspect, very short and rather shrunken. He had been a writer of sorts. I say "had been," because no ink had now flowed from his pen in what would have been for an ordinary person a whole lifetime, but Dr. de Castries had no truck with ordinary lifetimes. He had been born, it is rumored, near the beginning of the twentieth century and had known most of the legendary figures in the field: Ambrose Bierce, with whom his name is linked in a perversely intimate way, the brothers Thomas and George Eastman, T. O'Conor Sloan, the ill-fated Alvin Middlebusher, and (or so it has been suggested) Edison himself.

Like Dr. Fredericks, he had anecdotes to tell in which these names were prominently featured. But I noticed that each story had the effect of diminishing the person he was talking about— as if Dr. de Castries were determined to shrink them all, until each was no larger than himself. The effect was felt. Gradually, the persons clustered about him fell silent, had no questions to ask and no laughing comments to make. It was as if so many lights were being extinguished, one by one.

"Well," I said to him with an effort, determined to break the pall that had descended on the company like a wet blanket from the ceiling; "well, you have outlived them all."

He turned upon me a smile that reminded me, somehow, of wintry sunlight on the side of a clapboard house. "Sir," he said, "I have *buried* them all."

That remark, and the smile, deepened the rather disagreeable impression he already had made on me and I turned away. I didn't know then that I was to bury him.

The Magazines

The oldest title in the field and the one which everybody knows, even those who "don't read that stuff," is undoubt-edly Thomas Alva Edison's *SCIENTIFIC ROMANCES*. It was founded in 1917, supposedly by Edison himself, the first issue being dated March. The earliest stories were nominally written by the great inventor and often featured him as the hero, as they did in such serials as *Edison's Conquest of Time* and *Thomas Alva Edison—The Man in the Moon.* The immodesty of this was not much laughed at, because it was accepted as a kind of convention. The "Buffalo Bill" dime novels were still mak-ing their rather dim appearance at the time and Henry James (the son, not the brother, of the famous psychologist) was just beginning the popular novels in which he celebrated his own supposed exploits as the world's greatest detective. It is well known now that Edison's stories were actually written by his

publicist, Thomas Eastman, who had conceived the magazine as an antidote to the natural headline-gathering talents of Edison's so-called "rival," Alexander Graham Bell. Eastman wrote all the material himself the first few months—about 150,000 words an issue!—but shortly began making enough from his share of the profits to farm out stories to other writers. As a result the magazine began to diversify its contents and, as time went on, to become more sophisticated, so that its first boyish readers found they could still read it when they had become men. After Edison's untimely death in 1927, his name was not often seen in the magazine except on the cover and contents page. Tom Eastman ceased to be editor in 1922, following a rancorous dispute between him and Edison as to which owned the rights to the stories Eastman had written under his patron's name. There has been only one editor since then, the long-lived "Thomas Alva Edison, Jr." I suppose everyone understands that this is a "house-name," the man behind the mask being, successively, T. O'Connor Sloan, Joseph Edison (a grand-nephew), William F. Jenkins (like his supposed namesake, an inventor), Karl Fredericks and, presently, R. Knerr. The venerable magazine's masthead and general appearance remain the same today as when our grandfathers were reading it at the age of twelve, although its circulation has shrunk to about a third of its original 300,000. It is published monthly from New York, sells for 25¢ a copy and pays 2¢ a word for stories.

You will be surprised (assuming you are not a cog) to learn that *Edison's*—although I think I am right in calling it the most famous magazine in the field—is neither the most respected among the *cognoscenti*, nor the magazine with the widest circulation. The honor of being the most respected belongs to *Gulliver*, which is published in my own Philadelphia, and is still edited by its founder, Mr. Lewis Denholm, though much assisted by his son. It is smaller than its famous rival, both in size (being a mere 6 x 8½") and circulation (about 70,000), but it has been holding its own for half a century now. It is monthly, costs 25¢ and usually pays 1¢ a word for material, rarely more.

Despite this low rate of payment, the ambition of every writer in the field is to be published at least once a year in *Gulliver* and so be invited to the annual Fellow Travelers Dinner hosted by the magazine.

The publication with the widest circulation is *The Rocket*—more than 140,000, according to a statement tacked to the masthead. It is larger in surface area than *Edison's* but considerably thinner, having only eighty pages; it could pass as a tabloid if it weren't stapled at the spine. It is undisguisedly a juvenile publication, but grown men have been seen buying it at news-stands, no doubt for their sons. It costs only 12½¢ a copy, but since that one thin bit has to be laid out twenty-six times a year (a new issue appearing every other Thursday), its subscription cost is the highest in the field. But it also pays the best money in the field, 2¢ a word to beginners and up to 5¢ a word, or so it is rumored, to "popular authors."

These three are the only S-R pulps now being published. There have been others during the past century, but they haven't lasted. Among these were Munsey's *Outlands* (1937-'52), which was long on adventure but short on science; *Metafiction*, published in New York City by the eccentric Willard Huntington Wright and which lasted only five issues, all in 1947, although how it could have survived even that long, considering that its cover price was three bits, is a mystery; and, what is by far the most interesting of these ephemeral titles, Alexander Graham Bell's THE COMING AGE, which saw only two issues for a reason I shall shortly tell. Greene's *Adventure Magazine* publishes an occasional scientific romance, as does also, though less frequently, *The Bat*, which specializes in supernatural fiction. "Less frequently" for a curious reason: some readers of the magazine consider "esser-fiction," as they call it, to be a less respectable form of writing than supernatural fiction and complain bitterly of the contamination.

The Stories

You will have noticed, as you flipped through the pages of this book, that not all the tales I am reprinting tell of inter-planetary voyages (though some do) or of Octopus-men from another star landing on this world, usually in the immediate vicinity of a farm in New Jersey. No: some concern themselves with Overmen, time-travel (both long-wise and cross-wise!), moxons, Utopias, telepathy, lost civilizations and prehistoric men. A story of course must speak for itself, and most of these do; but I think a few words from me might add to the interest of one or two, and I would like to say something also about two stories I am *not* reprinting.

One of these last is a "cross-time" or "branch-line" story. There have been quite a few of these, but the first, and in my opinion still the best, was "The Owl Creek Branch Line," which appeared in the February 1947 issue of *Edison's* under the by-line, "Thomas Alva Edison, Jr." In other words, it was written by the editor, who was at that time William F. Jenkins, who must be given credit for inventing this type of story, a type unforeseen by the prophetic Verne and Wells of the last century. It is a railroading story, thick with atmosphere (an atmosphere rendered visible and almost palpable by the striking illustrations of William Beck), and it remains one of the most fondly-remembered stories in the field. It tells how Engine 88, desperately being shunted onto a branch-line to avoid collision with an on-coming passenger train, finds itself being shunted also onto a "history-line" that branches off from our history-line on January 1st, 1901: it is shunted into a world that has never heard of Tichnor's Complaint. You might think that this would be altogether a good thing, but, strange as it may seem, Edison/Jenkins didn't think so. Since Europe and America in that history-line did not lose one-half of their populations to Tichnor's at the turn of the century, they have become, by this time, horribly overcrowded, with the result that there is wide-

spread poverty, famine, depletion of livestock and other natural resources such as coal and petroleum, unspeakable diseases and decimating wars. Since that world did not receive that "grim and salutary Warning," as the Reverend Vance would have it, which *we* received at the beginning of this age, the secularism of the nineteenth century continued unchecked and even flourished; the old certainties gave way and there was a widespread demoralization, which took many disconcerting forms. It is true that many of the famous men and women whose loss to Tichnor's we bewail—Mark Twain, Kipling, the James brothers, A. Conan Doyle, Teddy Roosevelt, Queen Victoria, H. G. Wells—were spared in that world; but there were also spared men whom we are the better for not having known, men who strove to give expression to all the voiceless rage of their confused world, such as Kaiser Volkermord of Germany and the Terrible Tsar, Ivan the Ironboot, of Russia. So that when, finally, the ingenious engineer, Old Tate, finds a way to get the train back onto the right track—after a thrilling climax, with another crowded passenger train bearing down upon them, as before, for a head-on collision—when he finally, I say, succeeds in getting Old 88 back onto our "trunk-line," some malcontents aboard her, most notably his sarcastic side-kick Stoker Harrison, discover that this "little backwater of a world," as the Stoker calls it, is not such a bad place, after all.

I wish I could include the story here, but can't. You may be able to find it at your local free library, for it has been reprinted, believe it or not, in book form, the only S-R story to attain that honor until now: in Germelshausen's *Big Book of Railroading Stories* (1977). Unfortunately, the publisher of that book, Fields Osgood & Co., purchased all rights to the story and have refused me permission to reprint it again. In its place I have supplied another "cross-time" story, the lesser-known but warm and touching "Woman at the Crossroads," by H.-J. Augenblick.

I used a word above that may have puzzled you, "moxon"... which brings us to another long story, one that you *will* find in these pages. "Moxon" means "automaton" or "mechanical

man," like the chess-playing automaton at the recent World's Fair in Chicago. The word is taken, in fact, from the name of the inventor of such a machine in the story, "Moxon's Master," written about 1880—a machine that strangles its inventor when the man defeats it in a game, "on its painted face a tranquil and calm look, as of one who has just resolved a difficult problem in chess." This story was undoubtedly written by Ambrose Bierce, who had a life as interesting as any of his characters and who left it more mysteriously than most of them: he was found murdered in his hotel room in San Francisco in the summer of 1922. The identity of the murderer was never discovered, nor was the motive of the crime. The police concluded that robbery was not in question, since the murdered man's wallet and ruby ring were not taken; but a Pinkerton detective hired by the Bierce family developed a theory that something nevertheless had been stolen. An 8 x 10 square outlined in the dust of the table showed that a book, picture or some other flat object had lain there and, since Bierce invariably composed his writings on paper of that size, it was speculated by the Pinkerton operative that a manuscript had been removed.

Not very long afterwards, Tom Eastman, at that time still editor at *Edison's*, received in the mail the manuscript of a novel, *The Slaves of Moxon*, "by Ambrose Bierce and Thibault de Castries." He read it and delightedly accepted it, mailing the check to de Castries. It wasn't until some three weeks later that he noticed, while working alone in the office late one night in order to check proof, that the name of each author had been typewritten on a different machine, Bierce on a Smith, de Castries on a Bell, and that de Castries' return address, had been typewritten over another address obliterated by papermilk. Not having much confidence in his own suspicions, and having a deadline to meet, Eastman published the story under the names by which it had been submitted to him; but he mentioned the matter to the New York office of the Pinkerton Agency, which notified the Bierce estate. The Bierce people wrote de Castries demanding remittance of one-half of the $800 he had been paid

for the story and asking incidentally for an explanation: for no one in the Bierce family had known that Ambrose had been working on such a story—swore, in fact, that he could not have been doing so. But de Castries never replied.[3]

Eastman never publicized this business, but the incident became common knowledge in the field and there was naturally a lot of speculation about it. Some, pointing to the fact that Bierce had never written a novel, supposed that the story must have been written by de Castries, anyway, despite appearances. Others, remarking that de Castries had never sold a story written entirely by himself, that all his stories had been ghost-written, thought that the man must have hired Bierce to salvage an unpublishable manuscript. The most sophisticated theory was advanced by Peter Dunne, Chairman seven times over of the Yahoos. He deduced from internal stylistic evidence that *The Slaves of Moxon* had actually been written by one Howard P. Lovecraft, an obscure hack living in Providence, Rhode Island, who had "ghosted" several other stories for de Castries, all published in *The Bat*. Peter, who has made a career out of investigating such mysteries in his spare time (he owns the bicycle shop in which the Yahoos meet) believes that de Castries added Bierce's name to the script to ensure acceptance. Perhaps so. But there still remains a mystery, doesn't there?—namely, that 8 x 10 square outlined in the dust of the table.

Thibault de Castries had long been presumed dead when, in 1982, sixty years after the publication of *The Slaves of Moxon*,

---

3. An interesting side-light is that the Pinkerton man wrote a book obviously about this business, though thinly disguised as fiction: *Doctor Plagiarus*, as by "The Pinkerton Op," the first of a series of popular books under that name (and which, oddly enough, have been highly praised by the intelligentsia, although one would have thought that the subtle mysteries of the cosmopolite Henry James would be more to their taste). I am told by a reliable informant that de Castries sued but dropped the matter after a private interview with the anonymous "Op." Indeed, he seems to have dropped more than that—he dropped himself out of sight for some decades. Two moving pictures have been made from the book, the second (1972) with sound.

he walked into the clubroom of the Yahoos one Thursday evening—he was recognized by the astounded Lewis Denholm, who had met de Castries when he, Lewis, was a small boy—and he has been coming back about once a month ever since. The most conservative estimate of his age, *even then*, was ninety-two. He has never been known to wear anything but an absolutely black suit, a black "bow-string necktie" (which on close inspection proves to be a shoe-lace) and a broad-brimmed black hat.

But enough of Mr. de Castries for the moment. After all, he is not the only mysterious writer in the field. Another is Virgil Parham, who is mysterious chiefly because no one has ever seen him. During the 1960s he wrote a series of comic shorts for *Edison's*, mostly about a backwoods inventor, Melvin Mumm, who devises ingenious contraptions that invariably turn upon him with disastrous and hilarious consequences. These stories have been much praised for the author's knowledge of southern rural dialect, the characters being mostly poor whites and negroes.

Parham's manuscripts were all mailed from Hick's Corners, a small town in Georgia. Once, when Peter Dunne was traveling through that state, he stopped off at this village to scout out the author of "Mumm's Last Word," "Herman's Home-Maids," and, as he said, "other stories too humorous to mention." But, despite its being such a small town, no one seemed to know anything about him; Peter's inquiries about "the writer Virgil Parham" elicited bucolic stares. Straying outside of town (which was not difficult to do), he met a lady with an umbrella on a country road, who said, "Virgil? Oh, he's at the ice house. Just around the bend there." So Peter went around the bend, but found no one in the ice house except a sweating red-faced man in an undershirt moving some packing crates with the assistance of a negro. He asked the obvious question and the red-faced man indignantly, even belligerently, replied, "No, *I* am not Virgil Parham!" and Peter, a gentle soul, even though he does make puns, retreated, went back down the rutted road to catch the next motor-coach,

concluding that the lady had either misunderstood him or he had misunderstood her.

So it would seem. But the other night, as I lay in bed drowsily thinking over this and some other stray matters, I surprised myself by roaring aloud with laughter. A light had broken in my darkness. A possibility had presented itself to me—presented itself with such force that I positively felt for the moment like the Pinkerton Op or Henry James himself. Forgive me if I don't mention my thought more explicitly, partly so as not to stagger you and partly to respect what would seem to be the writer's legitimate wish for privacy.

The last Virgil Parham short was published in the April 1969 issue of *Edison's*. During the long silence that followed, Parham, unlike de Castries, was not inactive: he was brewing something rather potent in that Georgia back country. For in 1987 there was serialized in *Gulliver* a long story bearing his name. It was titled *Black on White*, and apparently had been rejected by *Edison's*. It tells of an expedition to Africa seeking to discover the origin of Man (a dangerous subject!) and finding something else almost as significant and even more fascinating. The leader of the expedition has invented a means of taking moving pictures of events that have occurred in the past at any given site, no matter how long ago—and, by the way, the explanation of how this is done is startlingly plausible: one wonders why Edison didn't think of it—and what unreels before his astonished eyes is the living record of a prehistoric *negro* civilization, a civilization of high, scientific and cultural attainments, *supported by white slaves!*

The novel is told in alternating chapters, one series detailing events in the camp-site in present-day Africa, the other narrating at first hand events in that very ancient society. There are two heroes. One is the intellectually audacious leader of the expedition, the other the humane ruler of that long forgotten but once-glorious world, a moral genius of the stature of Lincoln, who is attempting against great opposition from his own party to liberate the slaves. The interest of the present-day chapters is that some member of the expedition is attempting to suppress

the Discovery by murdering, one by one, the other members. Can it be the brutal and benighted Boer, Eugen van der Veldt, who may not want the world to know that such a thing as the enslaving of whites by "blacks" (as he calls them) is, or ever was possible—with its obvious implication that negroes are not inherently inferior to whites? Or can it be the mysterious Anglo-Indian Jameson Neville, who may have his own reasons for not wanting the world to know that a colored people had enslaved whites for four-hundred years? Or could it be...? But never mind. The climax comes with the freeing of the slaves in that ancient time and the simultaneous, so to speak, detection of the murderer in this. The way in which these two plot-lines are worked in together at the end, the discovery of the murderer being made to depend upon the successful freeing of the slaves, is highly ingenious, and the means by which the author contrives to have the two heroes confront each other, as it were, at the climactic moment simply cannot be too highly praised. Unfortunately, the story is much too long to be reprinted here. It ran through eight issues of *Gulliver*, and it is much to the credit of the Messrs. Denholm, both *père* and *fils*, that they saw the tremendous interest of the story, despite its awkward length and unusual theme. The only consolation I can offer is that you very likely can find the installments (June 1988-January 1989) in any of the Holmes Back Issue Magazine Stores, at least one of which can be found in any good-sized town.

Only one of our stories features "The Father of Scientific Romance" himself—I think we can call him that with some justice, without slighting the crucial role of Thomas Eastman. I have not chosen any of the long stories from the early issues of his own magazine, which featured him as the first-person narrator, but have taken a shorter piece from the short-lived publication of his "natural enemy," Alexander Graham Bell's *THE COMING AGE*. This is a novella titled "Edison's Greatest Invention," by "Menlo Park." Although it begins as a dead-pan denigration ("Thomas Alva Edison, the World's only inventor, sat alone in his laboratory and wept, like Alexander

(not Graham Bell), for new worlds to conquer. A bell rang somewhere, faintly, perhaps at his elbow"—in reference to his deafness. ("Was it that diabolical invention, the telephone?")—although it began, I say, in such a fashion, the writer of the story not only became progressively more fascinated by the scientifically speculative aspect of his story but there crept into his writing a note not only of respect for Edison but even of affection. Everyone recognized this...everyone, that is, except Edison. Ordinarily phlegmatic and insensitive in personal relations, he was embittered by the suspicion that the story had been written by his former friend and associate, Thomas Eastman, who had done the earlier "Edisons" in his own magazine. The story is now widely thought to be one of the best of the early Science-Romance tales, though not many have read it. For the affronted Edison sued and the Court forced the owners (principally, George Eastman, Thomas's brother) to recall all unsold copies of the first issue, in which the story had appeared, and to publish in its second an apology. That second issue was also its last; for the ever noble and generous Alexander Graham Bell—now, *there* was a man!—who had had nothing to do with the so-called feud with Edison and obviously hardly knew such a thing was supposed to exist, withdrew permission to use his name and put a stop to the magazine. I am proud to publish here this exceedingly rare document from the history of S-R, with the express and very kind permission of the present executors of the Edison and Bell estates, who have also granted me the right to publish five other stories from *Edison's* magazine, including *The Slaves of Moxon*, and one other from *Bell's*.

A Few Acknowledgments

I decided to obtain those permissions in person and telegraphed for an appointment, which was granted. I took an afternoon train into New York City and on the way browsed through some back issues of *Edison's*, partly to divert my mind from a

decision I had to make and partly in hopes of discovering still another forgotten masterpiece. Thoughtfully glancing up at one point, I became aware that the middle-aged couple sitting opposite me were half-scornful of, half-amused by, my choice of reading matter. That is to say, she was scornful, he was amused. The magazine I was holding had a cover, by Poke, depicting a chrysanthemum-man locked in a death struggle with a space-suited tortoise.

"I bought these for my son," I heard myself explaining. "Naturally, I always monitor what he reads, so I thought I'd better look through them before placing them in his hands."

I was immediately ashamed of my pusillanimity. I had meant the remark as a kind of a joke, but somehow the saving element of humor had separated itself out and tumbled to the floor and what remained was nothing more than a cowardly fabrication. I have no son, and as yet hadn't even a wife...and what woman, I asked myself, would want to marry such a poltroon? And what made it worse was that the two persons I had tried to propitiate said nothing but continued looking at me in much the same fashion as before, except that her scornful smile was now touched with amusement and there crept into his amused face a trace of scorn.

I pretended to go back to perusing my magazine. Pretended... for I found I couldn't now lose myself in it. I know it's absurd, but I was conscious every moment that that man and woman sitting opposite were studying me. And that wasn't just my fancy, either, for every time I glanced up I saw those same amused, scornful faces, faces without embarrassment and without pity. It took another hour for the train to reach the 42nd Street Depot, and that hour was one of the longest I've ever spent; for I was writhing with self-contempt, contempt for the trashy magazines piled on the seat beside me, and for *them*, my silent judges. "They're probably Millerites," I told myself. "They think the world is going to come to an end at 11:22 A.M., Thursday next, so there's no point in reading about the future."

But when we got off the train at the Depot, I saw that they

were met by a chauffer and a motor-car, a late-model Selden. They were not likely, then, to be Millerites, as the members of that enlightened order are drawn exclusively from the lower social levels. No, these were wealthy, educated folk who despised my reading on other grounds. Oh, well...I shrugged the matter aside and took a cab downtown to my favorite New York haunt, *Pfaff's Beer Cellar*, for dinner. But the sparkle seemed to have gone out of Bert's beer, the steak was flavorless, and the talk I heard from the literary and theatrical people seated at the tables around me sounded in my ears unpleasantly loud and coarse. I was conscious also that I was badly dressed. My suit was too dark and too heavy for summer and my hat was villainously dark. I felt like...what did I feel like? The answer flashed into my head: I felt like Thibault de Castries! Absurd! How could anyone—except Thibault de Castries—feel like Thibault de Castries?

I was half-inclined to give up the book altogether as a bad job, but I shrugged that aside too—after all, I had come all this way and might as well go through with the interview—and took a trolley across the bridge. I hired a bicycle from Tulliver's at the car-barn and pedaled myself through the rural, or, rather, the landscaped, Bronx, "The Garden Spot of the World," as it calls itself, towards Silverwires. I pedaled on a lonely road that wound gently between two thick curving endless hedges. There were no street-lamps, but I didn't need them: the moon was so large and full as to seem positively bloated and the stars were as thick as...well, as thick as the crickets in the hedges. An automobile approached me from the rear, its powerful headlights arrogantly sweeping the road for a hundred yards ahead and exposing me briefly to a pitiless glare. It hooted—unnecessarily, I thought, as I already had swerved to one side—and, looking back, I saw a lonely, defenseless creature reflected in its windshield. It roared past me, a heavy expensive sedan, a chauffer at the steering-wheel, two shadowy figures in the passenger compartment, and, contemptuously showing me its backside, disappeared around a curve. The night was warm but I shivered; the bicycle wobbled

under me. That automobile...it had been a Selden. And hadn't I recognized those two lumpish figures in the back? And wasn't it going in my direction? Towards Silverwires? What if...what if Mr. and Mrs. Edison should turn out to be that middle-aged couple on the train? Suddenly, that seemed almost irresistibly plausible. So much so that by the time I had reached the famous estate and had leaned my bicycle against the ornate gate, I had convinced myself completely of the truth of the presentiment.

But we can't always predict the future, not even those of us who read "S-R." The Mr. and Mrs. Edison who so graciously greeted me proved to be a young couple—or young enough, anyway, although Mr. Edison has a shock of prematurely white hair that makes him look startlingly like his famous ancestor. In a matter of minutes they made me feel as though I had known them for years. I felt not like an editor importuning permissions, or a reporter interviewing them, but like a guest, and they spoke confidentially and without stint. I had supposed that the magazine bearing their name would be of little interest to them. I had even supposed that they would have the usual amused attitude towards it, but no such thing. Although Mr. Edison naturally delegates responsibility for the publication to a professional editor, the very capable Rudolph Knerr and his staff, I found that both were habitual readers of it—what is more, they have a subscription to *Gulliver* and even to *The Rocket!*—and Mrs. Edison was as enthusiastic about Science-Romance as any teen-age boy. You'll be surprised.... No, you won't either! You won't be the least surprised to learn that I felt the most tremendous relief and gratitude.

We talked in Mr. Edison's study, before a giant fireplace with a roaring fire (the French windows thrown open into the spacious lawn, so that we wouldn't become oppressively warm). We talked, in that warm and friendly setting, the firelight glinting on our brandy glasses, the white-haired Tom Edison leaning against the mantle, the dark-haired Alexandra seated near me, of many things: of the field's past and probable future, of the supposed feud between Edison and Bell, of the

mysterious laboratory explosion that had killed Thomas Alva Edison and about which the present Thomas Edison has a rather grim theory; about the Boorman scandal, the Bierce murder, and (strange that his name should come up!) of Mr., or perhaps Dr., Thibault de Castries. I notice as I write that all this sounds distinctly unpleasant, but it didn't seem so at the time, partly because of the genial warmth of atmosphere my hosts cast about me and partly because we spoke of many pleasanter things too (such as my favorite writer, H.-J. Augenblick, whom they also both knew and liked).

I had to leave shortly after midnight, to catch the last trolley back to my hotel in Manhattan. They walked down with me to the gate.

"The air is like wine," said Tom.

"Yes," said Alexandra, "and it's given the moon a glow."

As I trundled away on my bicycle, I looked back and saw the two of them standing in the moonlight, their arms about each other, looking up at the stars. It was like an illustration out of *Scribner's*, so perfect that I smiled. There they were—the great-great-grandson of the inventor of the phonograph and the great-great-granddaughter of the inventor of the telephone. The famous, if rather one-sided, hereditary feud was now resolved, and resolved as in the old books, by the love and marriage of a new generation.

I don't suppose I had gone another fifty yards down the curving road when I glanced back for a last look at the rambling old house with its many gables...and collided with someone, whom I not only staggered but quite succeeded in knocking down. This someone cursed me volubly, with more vehemence of feeling than it had been my privilege to hear before. I'm not sure I recognized all the words he used—I would like to think I didn't—but I did recognize the voice.

"Doctor de Castries!" I cried. "My apologies!" I was off my bicycle in an instant and helping him to his feet. "But...but what are you doing...walking...in *this* neighborhood...at this hour?" I confess that I felt a thrill of something like superstitious fear.

His being here was so very unexpectedly, the Edisons and I had been speaking of him so very recently and so very pointedly. It was as if he had sprung up out of the dark earth in answer to our call.

"I can walk where and when I please, sir," said he, bristling his cane as if to strike me, but not doing so. "This is my neighborhood too and I am taking my nightly constitutional."

"Your neighborhood too?" I repeated, like an idiot. I glanced back—I couldn't help it—at the house I had just quitted. He turned his shadowy face in that direction, then back towards me and I caught the gleam of his eye under the black brim of his hat. A chill sank through me. I turned and, moving a little stiffly, picked up the bicycle from the road, along with my scattered wits. "Your constitutional, you say? No doubt, the secret of your health and long life." I was positively afraid of him, afraid mostly for that handsome and gracious man and woman I had left in the house back there. "It's the reason you have buried so many of your...." I deleted the word "enemies." "...so many of your friends."

He stood there a long moment, his black suit vampirishly drinking up the moonlight. "Yes," he said, "and I shall bury many others."

I got onto my bicycle without another word and lurched away. I had gone about twenty yards when I heard him calling after me: "You have hurt me, you scoundrel! You shall hear from my lawyers!"[4]

For a while I was disturbed by this encounter. But only for a while—the night was just too delicious, and my contact with the Edisons had renewed my sense of strength. Laughter bubbled up in me as I pedaled. Laughter and a kind of defiant confi-

---

4. But he had no more the power of prophecy than I had. I was never to hear from his lawyers; nor they, or anyone else, from him—His housekeeper was to find him dead in bed the next morning. I learned of this only today, a month later, while perusing the columns of Cog/nizance, which had picked up the information from the pages of the New York daily, The Reverberator.

dence. Let him threaten! I would call Tom Edison (on Bell's invention) from my hotel to warn him, but very likely Thibault's malice was now too feeble to cause any real harm. I hoped so. But whether he was dangerous or not, that ignoble, superstitious fear I had felt a few minutes ago had quite vanished. He was a pathetic creature. I saw that now. And I saw that we must never allow ourselves to feel awe before such a man. If he had killed as many as Kaiser Volkermord or Ivan the Ironboot, he was still pathetic, still a withered clown. He was kept alive by spite, the spite of the untalented, the unelect: of those who have turned away from what George Eliot has called "the mystery and wonder of the world."

At the thought I too, like my recent hosts, looked up at the stars and a phrase from my reading, I think from Meinecke, struck me so forcibly that it might have been the stars themselves speaking: "That sense of the infinite which enables us to bear the finite." Yes. And it was that sense of the infinite which, in the final analysis, was the secret well-spring of Scientific Romance...and this was true despite the pulp paper, the bad writing, the garish covers, or any other distortion the inspiration might suffer in the process of expression. And, yes, I told myself, I would compile that book (*this book*) of Scientific Romances, after all. And—again, yes—I would propose to Helen-Joan that she change Augenblick to what she herself had sweetly called "the hopeful name of Newbegin."

I pedaled on. The moon lighted my path before me. And, you know, the Edisons had been right: the air *was* like wine. I took deep draughts of it until my bicycle reeled under me as if it were tipsy.

A REPLY TO L. RON HUBBARD

"Up there—
"God?
"In a dirty bathrobe?"

> —The last lines of
> Hubbard's 1940 novel,
> *Typewriter in the Sky.*

He sat writing in his study.

He wrote with an old-fashioned quill pen at an old-fashioned desk with a slanting top, for such was his humor today. From time to time he dipped his pen into a shimmering liquid that was like the essence of midnight.

He bent his curiously familiar face with its neatly trimmed beard and high-domed forehead over the desk, his shirt-sleeved arm resting on the left hand sheet of his manuscript (which was blank, for he never wrote on the sinister side). Over his shirt he wore a short velvet smoking jacket of a rich color; it was more than neat and trim—it was exceedingly smart. Below the jacket he wore tuxedo trousers and, on his feet, soft leather slippers, very black but with little gleaming highlights.

The room in which he wrote was somewhat old-fashioned too. In the shadows to one side could be seen a comfortable easy chair, patiently waiting for the writer before a flickering fireplace. On either side of the fireplace dim shelves of books rose to the ceiling and, before it, a low table held a plate of

apples, bread and cheese, and—a warmly glowing red spot in the darkness—a bottle of wine. On the opposite wall was a tall window, through which could be glimpsed, here and there, an arctic waste, an endless canopy of green leaves, a cluster of distant suns, a restlessly heaving sea and the clamorous cities of men. But nothing unquiet troubled the deep calm of the study itself, in which could be heard only the gentle crackling of logs in the fireplace and the crisp sound the pen made as it moved across the paper.

He wrote slowly but steadily, his pen never faltering. There was no perplexity in his face and no irony. Now and then his eyes were touched by shadow but never by doubt. Now and then his lips were touched by a smile in which there was not the slightest trace of conceit.

And when at last he rose and lay down his pen, there was not a drop of ink on his hands nor on his immaculate white cuffs.

ABOUT THE AUTHOR

ARTHUR JEAN COX has written many stories under many names, a few of which he thinks it best not to mention. Those he would gladly mention include "Say That He Still Lives!" and "The Spectacles of Jorge Luis Borges" (both as by Arthur Jean Cox), "Writers of the Purple Page" (as by John Thames Rokesmith), "A Prince of Snobs" (as by Arthur Pendennis), and "An Occurrence on the Mars-to-Earth Run #128, at Approximately 2400 Hours, 21 January 2038" (as by William Dean). He would also include in that favored category all the contents of this present volume, and, any and all future publications of his fiction by Borgo Press and/or Wildside Press.